To Dad f ♡
Your Curs

Christmas 1998

DOGS OF THE CARIBOO
And Other Stories

CONTENTS

Dedication

I have known them in many places. Some of them became a large part of whole chapters of my life. Some of them I knew only for awhile. Each of them returned to me more than I was ever able to give. To these totally unselfish friends, "Dogs of the Cariboo" is lovingly dedicated:

Jiggs	BiLou
Captain Midnight	Ricann Lou
Patsy	Penny
Billy	Queen
Snick	Johnny
Punch and Judy	Flip
Bounce	Apache
Sook	Sands
Fluff	Jack
Smudgy	Ike and Mike
Ethel	Cat Man Do
Benecia	Shadow
Ruth	Plaid Cat
Little Joe	Kerry
Ticki	Al Nice
Jasper	Boss
Pet and Tops	Bells
Bill and Bob	Charlie Brown
Hope	Scrim
Charlie	Tiger
Tweetie Pie	Honey Bunch
Hannibal	Bruce and Lady Dog
Corky	Patches and Sands

Dickie	Sarge
Gidget	Maxeen
Barney	Silver
Thai	Little Orvie
Job	Simi
Mamacita	Squeeky
Niño	Buster
KeeKee	Goldy
Zamize	Smoky
Maya	Bobby
Alex	Yshtka
Popeye	Sybil
Tika	Miss Halloween
Pogo	Patton
Katrinka	Mister Blackberry
Tinker	Tippy Tim
Sheba	Mister Bones
Muggs	Sake
Popcorn	Sable
Snuffy	Cody
Sage	Pooh Bear
Sam	Libby

Acknowledgments

I acknowledge with gratitude the help and encouragement I have received from my family in writing this book; most particularly, my husband Bud. This is his book, almost as much as it is mine. He is sustainer and first listener of all that I write, contributor of many beneficial suggestions, and source of the wonderful story of Buster.

I warmly thank my good friend, Teena Bryan, who has not faltered in her encouragement since the days when Dogs of the Cariboo was no more than an idea. My special thanks to those who read the first completed manuscript: the late William Arnoldy whose memory I cherish; Rena Stevens; Malcolm Berko; and Gretchen Cain; and for the invaluable suggestions they made along the way.

I will forever be grateful to my literary agent, George Ziegler, who has worked diligently for a book in which he expressed his faith from the very beginning.

My deepest appreciation lives for those veterinarians who unselfishly cared for these animals and gave their time and talents and advice: the late Doc Hall and Dr. H. D Schoonover, of Findlay, Ohio; Dr. William Bone, now of Clinton, Kentucky; Dr. Don Howell, Seminole, Florida; and Dr. Gwenneth Hall, Clearwater, Florida.

In the absence of a complete listing of the organizations which routinely care for lost or unwanted animals, I give my heartfelt thanks to those of which I have personal knowledge: the SPCA of St. Petersburg, Florida, and the Humane Society of Clearwater, Florida, and their host of dedicated volunteers.

Suddenly, there is a rush to print date, and I pause just long enough to thank the publishers, Steve and Sandy

Mundahl; Krista Mundahl, who typed the final copy; and Editor Henri Forget, undoubtedly the best there is. I thank my friend Lil Cromer for the keen pair of eyes and the heart with which she checked and critiqued the galleys. Where would any writer be without the likes of such people!

During the many stages of this book's coming to life, I was thrilled but not necessarily surprised when, time and again, circumstances opened a door or provided an answer or an opportunity just when it was needed most. At a time when the outcome seemed uncertain and I needed a pick-me-up, Roy Peter Clark, a writing teacher at St. Petersburg, Florida's Poynter Institute, speaking to Pinellas Authors and Writers, reminded us that circumstances are God's sealed orders. That may have been the most delightful "circumstance" of all.

Introduction

Recently, a friend asked me when it was that my deep caring for animals began. I had not considered that question before, but I thought for only a moment and answered, "It began with a dog named Jiggs."

A few pages from now, you will meet Jiggs, a dog with no memorable heritage, no great beauty, no particularly noteworthy intelligence. Even so, he possessed some marvelously lasting quality which is much more difficult to fathom than my friend's original question.

The events which had interrupted my childhood at the time I met Jiggs were neither understandable nor explainable and they must have made suspect the actions and intentions of the people around me. Jiggs, on the other hand, exhibited a sense of exuberant well-being and trust and security which translated to a young child as happiness. Without offers or promises on the part of either of us, we shared a joyful time. More than all the kind words and generous deeds of people, the loyal presence of this first dog of mine may have pointed the way to my journey to belonging.

The lifetimes of other animals overlapped and followed his, for animals have continued to be an important part of my life. None of them has ever betrayed what I learned from Jiggs. An animal does not deceive. An animal accepts the best or the worst that happens and goes on, unspoiled and unsullied.

Now, from memory, from recordings, from old letters, I have drawn the true stories which follow.

Every animal I will introduce has lived and touched my life, or the life of someone close to me, in some meaningful way. Every person is real; and, to the very best of my ability, I have described the places where the stories actually occurred. No names have been changed. No fictitious persons have been added.

When it has been necessary to construct conversation, I have done it with consideration for the times and a close and kindred feeling for the characters involved and the places they inhabited.

Remembering these animals and these people in this way is my loving memorial to each of them.

I hope you will enjoy their stories.

Mary Gentry
Largo, Florida
August 1996

ix

DOGS OF THE CARIBOO

Part I

The second week of May was a good time to be getting away from Florida. Aside from the excitement I felt about the adventure which lay ahead of us, I was glad to escape the harsh summer heat and the frightening electrical storms which would soon begin to develop and move inland from the Gulf of Mexico.

A few months earlier, when the prospect of visiting a private gold mine in British Columbia had arisen, I scarcely knew where that Canadian province was located. My husband, Bud, hoped to be allowed to help with the mining operation, while I would be an unpaid cook and housemother to the crew. Gidget, the orphaned black and white cat we had adopted, was to go along as mascot.

The fishing vessel *Bearcat*, source of our recent livelihood, had been sold and delivered to her new owners. Mail delivery had been put on hold and lawn service arranged. The 1968 Chevy, bought new the day we were married five years previously, was loaded to its rafters with clothing, cooking supplies and utensils, and an endless assortment of items I knew or guessed we might need for a far northern summer.

Now, I looked back only briefly at the locked and

1

shuttered house disappearing from view as we turned the corner and left Lark Drive.

For two weeks, we meandered northward and westward, across the length and breadth of the United States, stopping for visits with relatives along the way.

Just north of Bellingham, Washington, we felt encouraged when we saw there was only a short line of tourists moving quickly through the checkpoint at the Canadian border. Friends who often made the crossing had told us we should expect no problems.

After a hasty check of the contents of the Chevy, the officer asked us to come to the desk, inside. Questions about our destination and the length of our proposed stay were quickly dealt with; it seemed to be a pleasant exchange. Then, the examiner made a question of the word, "Occupation."

And my husband, although he was twice retired — first, from the United States Army after twenty years' service and two wars, and a second time after five successful years as a commercial blue-water fisherman — replied, from the honesty of a work ethic rooted deep in his Great Depression boyhood, that he was "unemployed."

"What has been your past employment?" the examiner wanted to know.

"Sergeant Major, United States Army, and, until a month ago, commercial fisherman, sir," answered Bud in his best, and unforgotten, soldier's manner.

Excusing himself, the examiner went to a corner office where he huddled briefly with a higher authority. Then, as other travelers, at other windows, were being sent smilingly upon their way, Bud and I were ushered into that corner office and invited to have a seat.

Again, we were asked about our destination, length of

stay, and the purpose of our visit to Canada. Bud said that we had been invited by friends to join them for the summer near the site of property they had leased to search for gold on the bottom of a lake.

Would we be employees of these friends, the officer wanted to know, and my husband told him, "No."

Did we have sufficient funds to cover the time of our visit? Yes.

Did we own a home at the permanent address we had provided? Yes.

Had Missus Gentry ever been employed? I told him that I had been an employee of the United States Departments of Army and Defense, the State of Louisiana, and the Parish of Calcasieu, Louisiana. Smarting from what I felt had become an unnecessary examination of honest and worthy United States citizens, I added that I had never been fired from a job and that my government had, for the duration of my employment with them, granted me a Top Secret Security Clearance.

The officer did not seem impressed.

In what seemed to be, surely, the gruffest voice he could muster, he said, "Mister Gentry." And he looked long at my husband.

"Missus Gentry," he said, and turned his look upon me.

And then he seemed to look at the two of us as he made the pronouncement, "You are not to seek employment while you are in Canada. I repeat; you will not be employed. You cannot. You must not be employed while you remain in Canada. If you are, we will know it. We will send the Royal Canadian Mounted Police, and they will arrest you, and they will put you in jail. In that case, your United States citizenship will not be of help to you. Is that clear, Mister Gentry?"

3

Bud's spine visibly straightened another inch and, chin severely tucked, he replied, "Yes, sir."

The officer's next question was, "Is that clear, Missus Gentry?" and I told him, "Yes."

"You may go," he said. "We hope you enjoy your visit to Canada."

Inwardly seething, I walked with Bud from that officious man's presence and crossed the parking lot to our waiting car. After a reassuring hug from my husband, I took Gidget into my lap and allowed her gentle purring to soothe my spirit.

It would have taken very little argument for me to agree to our immediate return to the United States, but people were expecting us and Bud Gentry's word was as good as a bond.

Free, but considerably subdued by what I would henceforth think of as the border guards, we drove for some miles north before we began, again, to enjoy the scenery and the prospect of our summer's adventure.

Even so, every northward mile took us farther from the warmth and comfort of home, and deeper into a country where I did not feel welcome. By the end of the day we had covered four hundred miles, along the Thompson and then the Fraser rivers. Late in the afternoon, we reached Quesnel, the last city on our route.

In retrospect, I had a feeling Bud's statement that he was out of work, rather than that he simply might be retired from it, had an adverse bearing upon the way the customs officials had viewed our other declarations. It would be some time, however, before I would sort out the combination of circumstances which may have resulted in our cool reception.

One of the pieces of the puzzle had to do with some of our countrymen who had entered Canada before us. The area around our final and remote destination — Wells, British Columbia — had often been chosen by American "escapists," many of whom, after arriving there, lived a vagrant lifestyle, grasping only from time to time, at some temporary means of support. During the summer we would come into contact with some of these people and begin to understand why the Canadian government might not welcome others they perhaps feared might be like them.

Furthermore, one look at our five-year-old automobile, loaded as though we might be leaving home forever, may have been enough to account for our unwelcome reception at an otherwise friendly neighbor's border.

Completely unknown to us, there existed another element in the then-current state of labor unrest among Canada's own commercial fishing fleet, working offshore in the Pacific. Within a couple of weeks of our arrival in the country, we learned that it had been necessary to send out federal crews to take over the duties of striking fishermen. Perhaps their knowledge of that developing problem caused the border people to look askance at Bud's recently ended business as a saltwater fisherman.

In Quesnel, at an elevation of 1800 feet, the air was crisp, as springtime struggled to take hold. We toasted the chill from our bodies in a sauna at The Twins Motel and enjoyed a good night's sleep. The next morning we shopped for fresh produce and other last-minute supplies. At the Billy Barker Inn, a hotel dining room which seemed to have been overlooked by time, we savored a beefsteak meal well worthy of these twenty plus years' memory. Then with our last "town cooked" meal under our belts, we set out upon the last leg of our journey into the mountains.

Forsaking the highway at the northern edge of town, we began to climb a narrow roadway through the trees. With the crossing of a small bridge, and then a sharp turn to the left, Quesnel was gone from view, with its lumberyards and pulp mills, and its broad valley where the Quesnel River, flowing down from the mountains, meets the deep, swift, and beautiful Fraser.

Here, there was no concern for any compass direction, for the road turned and climbed, turned again, and dipped before the next climb through the towering spruce green forest. Now and then, as we traveled a stretch of road which clung to the outward side of the mountain, we looked across greening valleys, spotted with the lighter green of leafing deciduous trees. Homesites were few and far between.

With each rise in elevation, the temperature dropped lower. A cold, misting rain closed in upon us, clinging to the car's windows and obscuring our view. We found ourselves wrapped in a cold, gray cloak of dampness as the forest pressed ever closer on either side of the narrow, rutted road. Gidget left her carrier on the back seat and came forward to curl between us for warmth and, perhaps, for some sense of security.

At a place called "Cottonwood," the road grew straight, crossing a bleak, high prairie. Located just beyond the Swift River, all that remained of a former way station was a single building, refusing to give in to the moldering of time.

Further on, we came upon "Wingdam," where long ago a migrant Chinese named Wing, venturing north to seek his fortune, had stopped up a stream in an effort to capture the elusive golden metal. The miner's shack and a sign bearing the name were all that remained of Wing's Dam.

Soon we were again in the forest and, on this final fifty-five miles of our journey, the road was bleak or beautiful, carefree or troublesome; sometimes scary. At a black-marled ravine called Devil's Canyon, we found a crew standing by with machinery to winch our car back up to the highway, if we should slide off the road and tumble down the

6

embankment which disappeared in a maze of treetops. This knowledge, somehow, did not have the reassuring influence I'm sure was intended.

When we had safely reached a height of some 4200 feet, the roadway ceased its roller coaster climb, ran smoothly for a short distance, and then, for a mile and a half, made its way over a gradual rock-strewn descent. There the Chevy topped a small rise, slurred around a muddy bend, missing a broad pool of water which had eaten most of the roadbed, and paused at the crest of a broad mountain valley which had not yet grasped to its bosom the summer we had left far behind.

At the turn of the century, adventurers had come to these mountains and valleys from every corner of the continent — some, even, from beyond alien seas — to dig and wash and sift for gold. For richer, for poorer, most of the miners had left, but the name they gave the place had endured. Now, on this liquid, sun-hidden day, we, too, had come for adventure — and perhaps for gold — to the land they had called The Cariboo.

* * *

In the center of the valley glowed a singular gem — the serene and shining Jack of Clubs Lake, large enough to accommodate a bush pilot's float plane, but small enough to maintain the valley's natural isolation.

On a bluff, high above the lake's far shore stood the deserted, rust red buildings of the Gold Quartz Mine, which had once provided life to the valley. Its towering mesa of gray slag, the only place around where nothing grew, was a grim reminder of the mine's past activity and man's lack of concern for a land he has drained of its treasure.

Awed by the beauty unfolding before us, we drove into a giant bowl greening with springtime, ringed by rolling mountains which almost hid the rocky peaks rising beyond.

A flat-lander by birth and — until now — by choice, I stared, speechless, at the scene which stretched to every point of the compass. High, and hard on my left, the fringes of a village straggled in a line about halfway up the side of the green bowl; an assortment of houses and a small church steeple, almost obscured by trees. Just beneath them, a narrow gravelled road climbed to meet the street those buildings occupied. It was hidden in greenery for awhile, and then appeared again at their level, near the top of the hill.

Out of the land rising north of the town, tiny Cottonwood Creek wandered into the valley and across its center, to deposit its meandering flow into the lake.

Near the lowest part of the valley, six or seven crisscrossing streets marked the place where prospectors had first platted a town and pitched their tents. Gravel from their diggings had been plentiful and the streets they'd built remained, but the houses which had gradually replaced the miners' tents were now a huddle of weather-beaten cottages. From the tiny chimneys of two or three of these wooden dwellings rose trails of gray smoke but, for the most part, the houses looked forsaken, uncared for; some of them, perhaps, long abandoned.

Quite near the creek, in a narrow street which lay between twin rows of the smoke gray houses, trotted a gaunt, dirty-yellow she-dog. Loose skin over her large bony frame told of her hard search for irregular meals, and I wondered just how wild she was and whether she suffered hunger and homelessness great enough to present a threat to our pampered cat.

Sagging breasts swinging wide, the she-dog loped around a corner and disappeared.

The road we followed skirted the cluster of old houses and climbed gently toward a peak rising some distance to the east.

8

Down that mountainside wound the zigzags of ski trails and tiny Lougheed Creek bubbled out of it, to tumble into a bed of worn brown rocks on our right, and then to hurry on to the Jack of Clubs Lake, now behind us. On the far side of the shallow streambed, the raw bank rose an abrupt hundred feet to the bluff of the Gold Quartz Mine.

Now, on our left, we finally approached our day's goal: six barracks-like, two-story concrete block buildings. They had been set there on the mountainside to house the Gold Quartz' hired hands when big business replaced the pick and shovel tent dwellers. One of these six buildings contained the rooms which would serve as our summer headquarters.

In a gathering dusk, we tumbled from the car, tired and cold. Immediately, our senses were assailed by the scent and the presence of a great shaded forest which had been living and dying since the mountains themselves had been formed.

I slept soundly that night, covers pulled close against the chill which seeped through and around the pane of the north-facing window. In the still hour of midnight, Gidget left her place at the foot of our bed and came, with the stealth of a stalking lioness, to share the warmth of my arms.

Early next morning, we set out for Seven Mile Lake, eager for our first visit to the property where the crew would work a placer lease during the brief summer ahead.

Just outside of town, we saw the she-dog, loping along the side of the road, occasionally pausing to sniff and trot on. Once she stopped, head atilt, ears pointing forward to listen. Pouncing, she snapped at a small rodent once or twice and swallowed the thing whole. Her scrawny body and pendulous udders clearly indicated the presence, somewhere, of a litter of puppies, and I wondered if their livelihood was dependent solely upon her roadside foraging.

The brief incident triggered my compassion for the yellow

she-dog, but offered no hint of the part her kind would play in my Cariboo summer.

Part II

Frequently, as I came and went about the village, I saw the yellow female investigating garbage heaps or loping along the roadside, but she always quietly avoided my approach. I came to think of her as Lady Dog. She was obviously a creature fallen upon hard times and little did I realize that in this cold, unfamiliar environment, it would take a very special event to allow me the acquaintance of even this seemingly acquiescent stray dog.

To the north, from my kitchen window, I could see the wintery mountains called Twin Sisters, rising to a height of over 6200 feet. In their embrace, some thousand or so feet below their peaks, lay Seven Mile Lake, just then shedding the last of its winter mantle. It was this lake upon which our friends and Bud would concentrate their summer's search for gold. On my first visit to the lake, on the first of June, I had found the soft gray paws of pussy willows, larger than any I had ever seen, pushing through the snow to announce the imminent arrival of springtime.

By the second week of June, a pair of loons had arrived after wintering far to the south. Mated for life, these birds had spent each summer of their adult lives on the lake, with the prospect of as many as twenty years of travel and homemaking and chick rearing together. Now, they noisily repaired their old nest at the far end of the quiet body of water.

Early one morning, I set off for that portion of the village which lay beyond the brow of the hill, above the sparsely populated area where I had first seen Lady Dog. Market basket over my arm, I hiked down the gentle slope and

11

crossed the little wooden bridge spanning Cottonwood Creek, which gurgled across the bottom of the big green bowl.

Climbing the tree hidden grade on the north side of the valley, I heard a strange noise coming from beyond the bend in the road at the top of the hill. It grew in volume and, by the time I reached the level of the upper village, I recognized it as the yelping and howling and barking of many dogs.

Rounding a turn at the top of the steep climb, I came suddenly into the broad, dusty street, where two small hotels, the Jack of Clubs, and the Wells, flanked a dinky cafe and an axe-and-lantern hardware store. Just past the Hong General Store, operated, now, by the descendants of a Chinese immigrant who had come here in the original gold rush, there was a garage, a post office, a Mountie station, and an Anglican church. This and little more made up the town's business district.

The noise I had heard as I came up the hill now filled the air with its discordance. I stared, mouth agape, toward the corner, a short block away, where the din suddenly took shape in the unlikeliest congregation of canines imaginable.

In a cloud of dust they descended upon me, a broad avalanche of dogs in an assortment of sizes and descriptions usually seen only at the most active of animal shelters. There were broad-chested Eskimo dogs, a delicate-faced collie, shepherds, a single yipping poodle, bewhiskered terriers, and motley odds and ends of mongrels, mutts, and curs.

At the front of this pack of some twenty or so animals, and obviously Boss Dog, was the most formidable canine I'd ever encountered. His coarse hair, like that of most of his cohorts, the color of mud-streaked pewter, matched the surrounding earth. His coat covered an enormous frame laced with hard muscle which flowed and caught and flowed as the big brute ran toward me.

The dog had the long reaching strides of a racehorse; his thick-padded feet came down like hammers with every step. The very size of his open, tongue-trailing maw and his flashing teeth might have been terrifying, if I hadn't been so thoroughly taken by the overall sight of the great animal which looked part wolf, part malemute, and, surprisingly, part laughing-eyed pet dog.

I probably didn't close my own mouth or take a decent breath until the lot of them had galloped past me, rounded the corner, and thundered out of sight down the hill I had just climbed. As they ran, they yipped and barked and yelped and snarled in a chorus which spread the sound of bedlam over the mountainside.

On future days, I would see the pack again and again, on one of their mad dashes through the streets of Wells or engaged in mock battle by twos or fives or sixes, or snarling over possession of some bit of roadside carrion.

Occasionally, I encountered clean, mannerly, well-nurtured dogs which lived behind doors in the village, and I saw other dogs resigned to a dull and featureless life, rope-tied in dooryards.

Then, at last, one day, I discovered Lady Dog's family of five fuzzy brown puppies, playing in the sun by the sagging door of a shed in "lower" Wells. Hoping they had not learned to fear humans, I tried to approach them, but they scurried, yipping, into the dark shed.

I had to accept the fact that these animals were an apparently unapproachable dimension in my growing picture of the Cariboo.

Part III

The six concrete block barracks which had housed crewmen during the heyday of the Rose Quartz Mine had been built to surround a rectangular inner court roughly the size of a football field. Placed as they were, around the edges of a slightly deeper depression on one side of the green mountain bowl, the buildings, now mostly vacant, formed a small community of their own. Reflecting that strange hunger among residents of the far north which cries for color to relieve the bleak and colorless winters, some imaginative artist had dyed the buildings in Easter egg colors of rosy buff, bright pink, and aqua.

Ours was one of the center apartments of the aqua building, which faced the steep palisade upon which the old mine buildings sat. We were separated from the minescarp by a narrow gravel roadway and the broad rocky bed of Lougheed Creek.

One chilly, sun-filled morning, I played with Gidget among the wildflowers growing profusely around the buildings. As the little cat leaped and chased imaginary mice among the giant dandelions and Indian paintbrush, I began to have that feeling of being watched which defies explanation but cannot be ignored.

Instinctively, my eyes scaled the nearby scarp to see, spying upon my cat and me, the great pewter colored beast I'd watched leading the pack of feral dogs about the streets and the countryside.

For only a long moment, he stood there, looking silently down at us. Then he simply disappeared, seeming to melt into the trees which had surrounded him.

At dusk one evening soon after that, as I loitered near the back door, looking into the gathering shadows, my sight was arrested by a movement at the far end of one of the barracks buildings on the down-side of the compound.

I inhaled a long whisper of breath and stood stock still as I realized the big Boss Dog was again watching me from the shadows. Motionless, we eyed each other for a long moment before I began to walk cautiously down the hill, palms open and held upward, whispering that he was a nice dog and a good boy, though I had no real reason to be certain of either.

I'm sure I didn't look away; I was too intent upon keeping eye contact with the dog, but suddenly the broad head with its wideset eyes was gone. It was as though I had failed to watch for a moment and, in the lapse, the dog had disappeared. When I rounded the corner of the building, he was nowhere in sight.

I was sure now that the big dog was checking me out and I hoped that his watching me might lead to a friendship. In this place I felt isolated for the first time in my life, and the fact there were animals which might be enjoyed inserted a ray of hope and anticipation into the loneliness of my days.

Although time and again I saw the Boss Dog watching me, he came no closer than the corner of the distant building or the shadows on the rocky face above Loughheed Creek. Then, hoping to entice him to within petting range, I left dinner scraps in a bowl near the back door on several successive evenings. The meal was always gone in the morning and I hoped the big dog was responsible for its disappearance, though I had not yet seen him near our building.

I continued to see Lady Dog as she made her scavenging rounds, often with her rambunctious puppies scampering along behind.

15

I'd read somewhere that growing fetuses, and later nursing young, exist on a me-first basis, which provides that when times are hard and food is scarce, they will leach the nourishment from a mother's body so they may grow and develop at whatever expense is necessary to the mother's health. Never was this exhibited more clearly than in Lady Dog's family of five, who grew round and full of life while she seemed to become thinner, more haggard looking, moving ever more slowly on her trips to find food at back doors and along the roadsides.

I longed to be nearer these dogs, to tussle and scratch the ears of Lady Dog and the big crossbreed and to cuddle the puppies, but they all avoided my close presence. It never occurred to me that in this land where I felt only too deeply my position as stranger and outsider among the human population, it would take a formal introduction to put me in touch with these half-wild animals if I were ever to know them any better.

My days in the Cariboo had reached into the warmth of late June when, one morning on a trip to the general store, I turned the corner at the crest of the hill to come face to face with a group of children, running toward me. I had seen most of them before, by pairs and bunches, but never so many together. Chinese, Eskimo, Native American, and Caucasian, the robust faces reflected origins of country and color quite as varied as the band of feral dogs. Furthermore, it was the pack of dogs they seemed almost to imitate, for they appeared to display no more discipline or purpose than the canines.

Leading this group was a delightful little Indian child, enjoying his fifth or sixth summer. His ebony eyes danced in a round, golden brown face, and his wide grin stretched across a set of gleaming baby teeth. He was running all lopsided and silly because, sunburned arms stretching to

16

encircle a shaggy neck, he was leaning into the shoulder of that magnificent beast which had been eyeing me from the distance and making off with my supper scraps.

"Wait!" I shouted as the ragtag flock, led by this unlikely pair, were about to pass by and disappear down the hill.

As one, giggling and squealing and shrieking, making noises they must have hoped sounded like the engines and brakes of the lumber trucks which rumbled daily down the road at the edge of town, the children slowed, made a wide arc in the dusty street, swooped back, and chugged to a stop in front of me.

We traded a tentative "Hi," and I asked the leader, "Is that your dog?"

"No," said the bright-eyed Indian. The word ended on an upswing, as though he were reserving his options.

"He ain't nobody's dog," volunteered another boy.

"Does he have a name?" I asked.

"Bruce," said the Indian.

I took half a step forward, my hand hesitantly extended, thought better of it, and asked, "Will he let me pet him?"

"What's your name?" Bright Eyes wanted to know, and I told him my name.

The Indian boy released his arms from Bruce's neck, took the dog's muzzle in both hands, the better to look him squarely in the eye, and said, "Bruce, this is Mary. It's okay if she pets you." The boy dropped his hands to his sides, returned his now-sober face to me, and said, "Okay; you can pet him now."

A short step, and I was standing next to the huge animal. His very size and stature made me wary, despite the glinting laughter in his eyes and the fact he was panting. (I have never seen a dog relax enough to do any serious panting when he was thinking about biting someone.)

17

As my fingertips made the first contact with the coarse hair of his head, his lolling tongue flipped the collected drops of saliva off its tip. Then, as though the broad, pink tongue were a ready sleeve, he used it to politely wipe his face.

The dog closed his muzzle and endured the cautious love pats I placed upon the broad expanse of his head. Nothing moved then but Bruce's eyes, which rolled upward to watch me as my hand rested for a long moment upon his forehead.

Suddenly, across my mind skipped the realization of how small my hand really was on that pewter colored head and that, if the dog were so minded, he could probably snap it off at the wrist in a single bite.

But Bruce had me in his spell and I wanted, more than anything else, to place my arms around his neck, as the Indian boy had. The dog might have sensed that, for he stood perfectly still in what may have been an invitation.

My notion to hug him was quickly replaced by another, however, which cautioned, "Maybe next time."

I withdrew my hand, stepped reluctantly aside, and said, "Good boy, Bruce." And then I turned and shouted, "Thank you!" to the children as they moved on down the street.

The last to leave were Bruce and Bright Eyes, but as they picked up speed and overtook their place of natural leadership at the head of the group, the boy shouted back, "You can pet him anytime you want to now!"

Part IV

July in the Cariboo was a time when long, sun-filled days and hurrying growth compensated for the shortness of the season.

Orange and red, lavender tipped petals of Indian paintbrush blossomed brilliantly along every roadside and beside every stream.

Dandelions nearly as big as teacups buttered great stretches of field and dooryard; their fast growing leaves were tender, sweet, and delicious when steamed and served with a sprinkling of crumbled bacon.

Ruby luscious rhubarb grew tall and thick around deserted buildings where it had been planted decades past, and only two stalks were needed to fill a five-person pie.

We soon accepted the strangeness of the half light which lasted until the middle of the night and became full daylight again long before time for our early rising.

Occasionally, we stayed up late to watch nature's fantastic show as the night came alive with the brilliance of the northern lights. Quavering and flashing, the aurora borealis expanded and withdrew, and grew and dimmed again, its kaleidoscope of color wavering from the northern horizon to the zenith and back again.

Although the peaks of the Twin Sisters, to the north of us, were periodically veiled with fresh snow, our meadows were green gardens where tall stems of nimbleweed waved rose-golden pennants in the sunshine.

The beauty of the Cariboo summer often wooed me from my need for sleep and I spent the time garnering memories of a lovely place I might never see again. Far into the strangely quiet half-dusk which lengthened the evenings, I would

19

sometimes walk about the village, pausing now and then, to watch the nighthawks and to listen to their peenting cries as they flew over the shore of the lake.

Or I might linger at the tiny Cottonwood Creek bridge to visit briefly with a little girl who came there, with a cane pole, to fish. She was the only black child in the village, and withdrawn.

During the entire summer, I never saw her with the other village children and, unable to shed my own feelings of outsideness in that strange place, I knew an immediate compassion for this lovely, lonely-seeming child.

In the yard behind our aqua barracks building, a set of five steps had been built beside the tall pole at one end of a clothesline which was for the use of the buildings' occupants. In winter, the line could be reached from these steps no matter how deep the snow became, and the hanging laundry could be moved toward the farther pole by means of a pulley, mounted just above. Now, the steps made a comfortable seat from which to watch the quiet evenings evolve.

Late on the very day I had been introduced by the Indian boy to the half-wild canine Bruce, the dog came openly to eat the supper I had put out for him. There was no hesitancy, no slinking toward the dish with tail hidden; no apology, either, for not having come sooner. He simply came up the hill to supper, as though that's what was supposed to happen on that day.

Afterward, by way of thanks, he came to me and nudged my hand into scratching his ears and I was beside myself with happiness.

He returned the next day, and the next, at suppertime, and the day following that. My apprehension about him melted away and our daily tussle after his meal became a source of mutual enjoyment. I was a child again, tumbling upon the

20

grass with a beloved and trusted pet, and my summer in the Cariboo took on a new glow in the light of the dog's friendship.

For the better part of a week, the big dog had been coming unreservedly to the food dish when, one evening, I found myself waiting for him long past his usual suppertime. Shadows broadened between the square concrete buildings as I watched for him from the steps under the clothesline.

At long last, his familiar shape separated itself from the shadows at the corner of one of the barracks, and he began to make his way deliberately up the hill.

Coming into the open, he stopped and turned to look back into the shadows, whining softly. A second animal came forward, head down, legs half bent, tail tucked close.

It was Lady Dog.

When she reached the great crossbreed, her ears rose in greeting. The muzzles of the two touched briefly. They sniffed. It was one of those unfathomable times when I just had to sit there and wonder, "What on earth are they saying to one another?"

A sudden wagging of Lady Dog's hindquarters seemed to loosen her shaggy tail, and it joined in a wild celebration, circling the air as the pair came bounding up the grade together.

Shoulder to shoulder, they approached the food dish. Lady Dog swallowed slather as she smelled the food. She nearly stepped in front of Bruce, but thought better of it and quickly resumed her former attitude of deference to the larger dog.

With a gentle pressure on her shoulder, Bruce nudged her toward the bowl. Still half-crouching, she began to eat as Bruce stood unmoving, obviously content to watch her take the food which had been placed there for him.

During what remained of the summer, Bruce never returned to the food bowl, though he would come to romp with me in the yard and almost daily he would walk beside me in the woods or through the town. I never had long to search when I would take some special kitchen treat and seek him out. Then, away from the bowl which he had obviously given over to Lady Dog, he would eat from my hand.

Lady Dog, however, came regularly to the dish Bruce had relinquished to her. I began to manage extra leftovers, for she quickly wolfed down whatever I put in the bowl. After eating, she would submit to my gently grooming her yellow coat, nuzzling my hand and thanking me with soft laps of her tongue.

I could not have guessed that she would seek another, more poignant way to repay my affection and my cupboard love before that magical Cariboo summer ended.

Part V

In the bright mornings of August I hurried to be free of the ancient kerosene-burning cookstove, the grossly inadequate water heater, and the ever present battle against the yellow-gray clay which every day found its way into my kitchen from the mountainside.

Escaping household chores with the excuse I wouldn't be there much longer, I would climb the nearby scarp on the far side of Lougheed Creek to explore the habitat of the scraggly raven which soared daily over the valley from the high crag. Or I might stop and hunker down in the shallow streambed to pan a dipping or two of fine gravel, making sure, in my innocence about gold mining, that a golden nugget had not washed from the mountain overnight.

If I left the breakfast dishes and went to the mountain very early, I might catch sight of deer, grazing the roadside, or the very special treat of a moose feeding, knee-deep, in some clear, meadow pond.   In the forest, I might see the smudgy red of a crossbill, feeding in the branches, or watch a wee sooty dipper singing, wren-like, as it flew just above the surface of a swift, shaded stream, taking insects from the air. Making its way beside the clear rocky current, the bird would suddenly walk into the water and, completely submerged, it would catch larvae, bugs, or small fry before walking out to devour its meal on the other side of the stream.

With only a few days left to find and store the precious memories, I hurried one morning to finish bed-making, barely aware of an unfamiliar noise coming from outside until Gidget began the throaty chatter which always meant that an alien had invaded her domain.

Through the window, I saw Lady Dog near the back door.

23

Beside her was the source of the strange noise. A round, brown puppy, that one which I had noticed was healthiest of her five, was yipping as it tried, in vain, to reach one of her sagging teats. None of the puppies had accompanied her to the house before and, anxiously, I left pillows unfluffed and sheets unsmoothed to join the two of them.

Running downstairs, I paused in the kitchen long enough to put together a bowlful of food, and hurried into the yard. While the mother ate, the hungry puppy hung at her breast, nursing ravenously. When the dish was empty, Lady Dog came to repay me with hand licking and nuzzling, and then turned her attention to the puppy.

She gave it a thorough bath and grooming and then, in an abrupt change of attitude, she snarled and snapped at the little dog, forcing it to lie down. With a final snarl, she turned and trotted off down the hill.

Puzzled, the puppy ran yipping after her and, again, she snapped at it, growled it into submission, and walked away. An unexpected mist covered my eyes as I realized her purpose and shouted, "No, Lady Dog!"

The sound of my voice brought her to a halt and she turned to look at me with a pleading I hated to deny, for it had become suddenly clear that Lady Dog had every intention of leaving this, the choicest of her litter, with me. She was determined; the puppy resisted; I knew I could not take the baby dog on the long trip back to Florida. "I can't do it, Lady Dog," I said.

Again, she came up the hill and nudged her puppy to a place near me. Full of sadness, I took her head in my hands and sat for a long minute with my face buried in the coarse fur of her neck. "I can't keep your puppy," I told her, and pushed her away.

I had grown too close to these dogs of the Cariboo, and

24

now my heart broke as I mustered angry sounding words to drive her and the puppy from the yard.

At last, her tail once again snugged to her haunches, Lady Dog led the way down the hill, her puppy following close behind. When they reached the bottom of the hill, Lady Dog turned again and tried, in that way animals do, to fasten her eyes upon mine but, fearing I might weaken, I hurried into the house and shed my tears into Gidget's soft, black fur.

I could not know the beginning or the ending of the story of Bruce and Lady Dog and their puppies, but theirs is the story of feral animals everywhere; the sad saga of those creatures cared for, awhile, and then deserted. Neither truly tame nor truly wild, bereft of human contact and protection, they face hunger, exposure, untreated disease and, worst of all, the propogation of new generations of misery.

Now, such animals had provided an indelible memory of my Cariboo Summer and I, too, must regrettably desert them.

Lady Dog and Puppy

JIGGS

At the south end of Main Street in the fair to middling size Ohio town sat an austere, but tree shaded, dark red brick building. Two stories and a live-in attic high, it housed the Findlay Home and Hospital. In the Great Depression year of 1930, the babies of only the county's wealthy families managed to be born there.

Almost exactly four miles north, at the other end of Main Street, on a patch of green lawn, stood another building, perhaps less welcoming in appearance than the first. Its dark red bricks, like those of the hospital, had been manufactured by local hands at the brickyard east of town, but this second structure had been built to serve people of a different station in life. A sign on the lawn said it was the Hancock County Children's Home.

Around the corner from the children's home, on Covington Avenue, was a two-story bungalow which, when I went to see it many years later, was covered with peeling green paint.

The best I can figure out, it was to that bungalow that Carl and Anna, in what was to be the last of many moves while their family was still intact, brought their brood of five children to live.

On the other hand, that green bungalow may have been only what was then called a "lying-in" home, where babies

26

were born when the parents hadn't the means to pay a hospital bill. At any rate — and there is written record of this fact — it was there, on a bitterly cold February morning, that Anna, attended by a local doctor, was delivered of me, her sixth living child. Another child, Elisha the Third, named for our Civil War great grandfather, had died while he was still a baby.

The first brief chapter of my life ended abruptly, a little over two years later. On a day late in May, 1932, we six children took up residence in the children's home. I may not know all there is to know about how we got there.

I've seen a picture of what was then my grandfather and grandmother's home, out on West Lima Street and, only recently, I heard that the county people came to that house, loaded the six of us into a car, and took us to the home.

But that's not what I grew up with, stuck in my craw, and that's the only way I can put it, because that's what it's always felt like to be told what I was told. Which was that our mother, after buying me a blue romper suit and a pair of black patent leather shoes from the Penney Store, walked the six of us up the front walk of that red brick building on North Main Street and left us because she didn't want us.

Papers were signed making us wards of the county, we told our mother goodbye, and watched, surely, as she walked away, down the sidewalk, alone.

Anna's tired body already carried her eighth child, who would be born in the third of the civically-owned red brick buildings, out near the Blanchard River and the Country Market, west of town. That building was the County Infirmary, often, in those days, called the poor house.

The pressures of the Great American Depression had destroyed another family. As the youngest of those six then-living children, I remember only scraps of my life on

27

Covington Avenue — or wherever it was we went to the home from.

There was a dusty dog which, most of the time, lay beneath a high porch, in a dark, cool place surrounded by wooden lattice. A rubber tire swing hung from the limb of a tree in the back yard, and I remember the older kids fighting with the neighbors over the right to play on the swing. I remember the blood and the shouting when my sister Fern Louise fell off the porch and broke her nose. I remember Carl holding me in his lap while he sang a song called "Pop Goes The Weasel."

And that's about it.

Events which occurred after we went to the home, however, are stubbornly stuck in my memory.

The red brick building itself was neat and whole and cared for. Just outside the kitchen door, in a grassless yard with a wire fence around it, there were swings and slides and a teeter-totter which never had to be fought over with neighbors; they were just for us children who lived there. A clean, fresh smell filled the home — clean and fresh like the matron's white apron and the sheets on the big bed my sister Fern Louise and I shared.

There were all the mashed potatoes I could eat, and big yellow peach halves which seemed to fill the plate in front of me. There was order to the days and quiet to the nights after all of the children were bathed and put to bed.

I would recall the smell of that cleanness and orderliness many times during my childhood; when I entered school, or when I went into some clean, well ordered institutional building. It always brought with it a feeling of safety and well-being.

The six of us had been at the home for two weeks when, just after breakfast one morning, there was the sound of a car crunching up the gravel driveway and stopping outside the back door. A tall lady with dark, happy eyes, came through the doorway, followed by a somber man, carrying his brown felt hat. The matron took the pair into the little office which belonged to Miss Orem.

Miss Hallah Orem was a skinny, crackly-voiced lady who came to the home almost every day and sat in her office reading papers and talking into the telephone. Sometimes she would stay after supper and play the piano, that marvelous piece of furniture which made the parlor such a special place. Miss Orem was always dressed up and always had bright red lipstick on her skinny lips. She wore spiffy looking shoes with pointy toes and spindly heels, and tiny little round eyeglasses, which she pinched onto her nose to keep them from falling off. While it was always the matron who was there to tell us when to go to bed and what to do while we were awake, it was Miss Orem, we knew, who was really boss of the home.

On the morning I'm talking about, the three grownups were in Miss Orem's office only a short while before they came out to where Fern Louise and I sat, washed and combed and wondering why we had been cleaned up so specially and told to sit and wait. The shiny black patent leather shoes felt strange to my small feet which had been accustomed to going bare, and I must have wiggled around a lot, trying to get comfortable, for I remember being told I'd have to sit still and behave if I wanted these people to like me.

Now, Miss Orem told us that we two girls were going to live with the smiling lady and the somber man on their farm, out in the country. "No," she said, in answer to the fearful questions of six fearful children; "not Evelyn and Catherine and Clayton and Thurman; just Fern Louise and Mary Ellen."

The two of us were placed in opposite corners of the back

29

seat of the tall, old, black Essex automobile and, waving goodbye to our brothers and sisters, we left the home. On the seat between us the man had placed a cardboard box containing a change of clothing, which was all that was ours. Thus began a long journey to belonging.

After a simple explanation that they would now be our mama and daddy, and we would be their little girls, the man and lady in the front seat talked in low voices which we could not hear well enough to understand.

Too small to look squarely through the window, I watched the telephone wires looping along between the poles, until my big sister told me we were going by something special. Then I hooked my fingertips over the window frame and pulled myself up to see the fresh green fields or the towering woodlots, the neat sets of farm buildings with broad spaces between them, or the fields with quiet animals standing in the shade of big trees.

It seemed we travelled for a long time. At last the car turned into a driveway beside a broad green lawn which sloped down past scattered trees to a gravel road and came to a stop at the end of a brick path. The man gently lifted me from the car and stood me upon the ground.

The barking of a dog came from the direction of the house and, looking toward it, I saw a large, smooth coated, black and white dog, bounding down the pathway, his long, skinny tail slapping the air as he ran. When he reached the place where we all stood, he stopped barking and his long pink tongue trailed from the corner of his mouth as he panted loudly. He looked as though he were laughing.

The dog quickly investigated Fern Louise and me, and then made as if to place his front feet on my new daddy's chest. "Get down, Jiggs," my daddy said, and the dog ran to me again.

I threw my arms around the dog's neck. He licked my face and, from that moment, it seemed as though Jiggs was my dog.

In the days and the weeks and the years which followed, I romped with Jiggs and talked to him, always sure, from his actions, that he knew what I was saying. I laughed with him and, sometimes, cried the tears of my little girl fears into the bristly hair of his neck.

With the big dog at my side, I roamed about the farm and learned the contentment of being outdoors and of discovering the growing things of the yard, the pasture, and the woodlot, with Jiggs always nearby to share them. We investigated what lived and grew along fence rows and roadsides. We chased through my daddy's tall perfect rows of corn, and gloried in the scent and sight of clover and alfalfa and timothy hay growing tall and blossoming.

The dog was never far away when I would lie on my back doing nothing more complicated than wondering where the clouds were going. When I lay on my belly, parting the grass to gaze, Gulliver-like, at the world hidden there, Jiggs would look, too, matching my own mood with quiet or excitement.

My new foster parents were good and loving people who would provide a clean, healthy, and disciplined life for all the years of my growing up. My sister, two years my senior, and I knew we were loved by these people, and we were taken into the larger families of each of them. But always, just out of reach and unchangeable, was the spectre of not having been kept by real parents.

Jiggs was my friend. No matter what I did, no matter how afraid I ever was of anything, no matter how lonely or sad or unwanted I ever felt, Jiggs never changed. He was always content to be with me, just because we were friends and because I was there and he was there, and it never mattered to

Jiggs at all that I had been given away.

I suppose it seemed nothing would change.

Jiggs and I had been best friends for nearly three years when I began to hear strange bits of conversation among the grown-ups, or they would stop talking as I came through a door or around a corner. People who knew Jiggs had always called him "good boy," and paused long enough to scratch his ears or swat him on the back as though they liked him. Now, all of a sudden, these people were walking the long way around my dog and sneaking looks at him out of the corners of their eyes, or just avoiding him altogether.

It was as though a dark cloud surrounded Jiggs, an awful cloud which grew bigger and blacker every day. Nobody would tell me what he had done to earn such treatment.

Each night now, before we went to bed, Jiggs was rope-tied in the woodshed. At unexpected times during the day, Daddy would ask, for no apparent reason, where Jiggs was. The dog would be called, and he would come to run in circles and look anxiously at us, confused because nobody wanted him for anything.

One morning, while Daddy fed and watered the livestock, I heard him whistling and calling for Jiggs. When he came in to breakfast, he made a fearsome announcement. "Jiggs isn't here," he said.

From the kitchen window, I could see the piece of old rope lying in the doorway of the woodshed, its end frayed and empty. Jiggs was gone, and he didn't come when we called him.

I stood at the gate by the side of the barn and called his name. I went to the fence at the back of the garden and looked across the fields, anxious for a sight of him. Running to the bottom of the sloping front yard, I peered into the woods which surrounded the maple sugar camp across the road, and called for Jiggs.

He was nowhere to be found.

Much later that day, when everyone else seemed to have given up, I saw my dog, limping slowly up the road toward the barn.

The breath I was taking in just then stopped in my throat. Hot tears welled into my eyes. "Daddy!" I cried. "Come here! Hurry up, Daddy."

Jiggs was bleeding from ragged cuts on his legs; evil wounds scarred his tail, and there were deep and ugly gashes on his hindquarters.

Bouncing against his body and dragging along behind him were the awful things which had caused his wounds. A horrid assortment of tin cans, their partially cut off lids sticking out at odd angles, clinked and clattered and slapped at him, their knife edges bringing new blood with every step. Binder twine fastened the cans together; a piece of the stuff circled the dog's belly and was tied to his tail so he couldn't get away from it.

I had heard men talk about canning a dog, but nothing they had said had prepared me for this sight of my suffering friend, and I ran to meet him.

"Don't touch him!" my daddy shouted. "He's hurt, and he might get mean." But I threw my arms around the dog's neck and my tears flowed into his fur, and I hated with a terrible passion every person I had ever heard say anything about such a terrible deed.

His apparent lack of sympathy for Jiggs seemed surprising as Daddy cut the binder twine and carried the disgusting cans to the junk heap behind the barn. Mama and I cleaned the dog's wounds with soap and warm water, and covered them with gooey Watkins' carbolic salve. Mama said if Jiggs didn't lick the salve off, it would help keep the flies away from the cuts.

I rooted through the stack of burlap bags in the woodshed and, finding a fresh one, made Jiggs a clean bed. Then, for most of the day, I stayed beside him and petted him, to keep him from licking off the salve.

A day or two later, eavesdropping, I heard the name of the farmer who had canned my dog. It was said he had found Jiggs trespassing on his property and had sent him home, confident the lesson would teach him where he belonged. It was apparently not the first time Jiggs had wandered beyond the line fence which separated the man's farm from ours.

That day, I stored away a grudge which stayed with me for a long, long time.

It was nearly thirty years later, on a summer day in 1974, that I went with Daddy to attend to some business at the First National Bank. From where he sat, Daddy saw the former neighbor, standing in line before a teller's window. "Well, looky there," Daddy said. "I haven't seen him in years." I went to the old man, told him who I was, and made myself swallow the guilt I was feeling about what I had in mind, because the former neighbor seemed glad to see me. Then I told him I'd never forgotten about his canning my dog when I was a little girl.

A look of remembering came over the man's face and for a long moment, I just stood there, looking back at him and saying nothing which might help him feel better about whatever he was thinking. Then I touched the old farmer on the arm and turned around and walked back to where my father was sitting.

It was the best I could do by way of finally putting the unforgivable incident to rest. I had got one thing out my of craw.

In the February after that summer canning, I turned six.

Another springtime arrived, and life on the farm assumed an urgency. As they did every springtime, 300 day-old White Rock chicks arrived from the hatchery in town. Velvet-coated, limpid-eyed calves appeared; we were told they rained down. And often, on cold mornings, Fern Louise and I discovered wriggling newborn Chester White piglets in burlap- bag-lined potato crates, behind the kitchen stove. Given a good warming, they would be returned later in the day to their mothers, waiting in their unheated farrowing pens.

In the shelter of the haystack in the back barnyard, docile, heavy ewes found pristine lambs, teetering on long, spindly legs, and wagging long, disjointed seeming tails as they nursed. Within a few weeks, these lambs' tails were "docked." Daddy said cutting the tails off wouldn't hurt because the lambs were so young, and it had to be done for their later cleanliness. He was careful to bury the cut-off tails deep in the ground lest Jiggs find them and learn to associate the taste of blood with the smell of sheep.

It was that year's early summer when, quite unexpectedly, one day, Otho Greenawalt came for a visit, bringing with him the feeling that something was very wrong.

Otho was a grown-up cousin in this family my sister and I had been taken into. I dearly loved him. He was fun to be with and always had time to talk, and to listen, to a little girl. He was an accomplished hunter and marksman, and often brought pheasants or rabbits, when he had been hunting in our part of the county. Cooking them, Mama would say that Otho, with a .22 rifle, could shoot a squirrel out of a tree when nobody else could even see a squirrel.

On this particular day, Otho didn't bring any game for Mama's skillet, though I knew he had been hunting, for I saw his rifle lying on the back seat when I ran to meet him.

From the moment of his arrival, there was a strangeness about Otho's visit. I was told to stay outside and play, while Otho and Mama went into the house, and I felt very alone and afraid, as though something terrible was happening inside the house or was about to happen, outside, where I was. I shared my uneasiness with Jiggs, and he licked my face, which always made it seem as though he understood what I was feeling.

In a little while, when Mama and Otho came back into the yard, my cousin was saying, "Well, I might as well get it over with." He called Jiggs to him, grasped the dog's thick leather collar, and led him toward the car.

"Where you going with Jiggs?" I asked.

"I'm going to take him hunting," Otho said.

Mama sounded sort of uncertain, then, as she interrupted her nephew to say, "Otho's taking Jiggs on home with him for awhile. Tell him goodbye."

It was as simple as that. I was certain there was something terribly wrong in what was going on but I knew better than to argue with Mama. I threw my arms around the shaggy neck of my good old friend, hugged him hard, told him goodbye, and watched him climb into the seat beside my cousin. And then I ran to the back of the house so I wouldn't see Otho drive away with my dog.

The years passed. Other dogs came and went on the farm, but nobody ever explained about Jiggs' untimely departure, nor did they explain why he never came back.

World War II came and Otho went off to an army camp and then even farther off, to the South Pacific. We exchanged the strange V-Mail letters which arrived as only small photographs of what had been written. The family wondered why Otho seemed to be working with the Air Corps instead of the Army, which had trained him. It would be long after the war was over before he told me some tests had showed he had a very special kind of ability to see and identify shapes and his officers had set him to work spotting enemy aircraft. I knew, as soon as I heard that, that it explained why Otho could shoot squirrels that other people couldn't see, but nothing had explained why he would have needed Jiggs for a hunting dog.

I enjoyed writing to this special cousin of mine, and was often tempted to ask him about Jiggs, but never did.

Eventually, the war was over, and when Otho came home, he made good his earlier promise that, when I was old enough, he would teach me to use a .22 rifle. We had gone to the woods one day, and under my cousin's tutelage, I soon graduated from just hitting a row of tin cans to firing at a can from one position until the can was driven clear out of sight.

Elated with success, I wanted to continue firing the rifle, but Otho said we needed to talk about hunting. He explained the usefulness and the dangers of firearms; he talked about safety and the wisdom of game limits, and promised to teach me, some day, to skin and dress the gamebirds and rabbits I would kill.

Encouraged by feelings of confidence and closeness with my cousin, at a pause in his teaching, I asked, "Will you tell me what happened to Jiggs?"

Twin wrinkles sloped down my cousin's forehead toward the top of his nose, as though this was something he'd already been thinking about. And then, Otho Greenawalt looked me squarely in the eye and said, "On the way home that day, I stopped at a pretty place in the woods and shot Jiggs. Uncle Frank had caught him killing sheep."

I pressed my lips tightly between my teeth and forced my eyelids wide to hold back hot tears. I was fifteen, then, too old to cry.

37

Otho picked up the gun and, together, we walked up the long cattle lane toward the house, both of us remembering a very ordinary black and white dog named Jiggs.

It would be many years before I fully realized what an important part Jiggs had played in my journey to belonging and, just as important, in fostering what was to become an immediate and lasting affection for every animal I would ever meet.

POPCORN

Popcorn and Ricann Lou

Doctor H. D. Schoonover's name had been familiar to me for as long as I could remember. Known simply as "Doc," he was a respected veterinarian who was occasionally called out to care for some ailing member of the farm's collection of livestock. Furthermore, he owned a string of spirited racehorses whose performance was legendary.

I met Doc in 1948, when for the first time, I went to the old racetrack at Fort Miami, near Toledo, to watch the ponies run. I knew one of his sometime drivers and, before long, names like Doc's ByLou and Princess had become as familiar to me as those of the pets at home.

After his retirement from the practice of veterinary medicine, Doc assumed full-time responsibility for the breeding and training, and a certain amount of pampering, of those horses on his rolling, white-fenced farm, east of Findlay, Ohio.

Doc and his wife, Ruth, took the trotters to pretty near every track within trailering distance, and the horses always did them proud.

39

Come the first week in September, people showed up at the county fair in droves: the farmers whose stock he'd treated, and all the other folks who knew Doc or knew of his reputation as a driver and a horseman. Spread across the grandstand or crowded up to the rail, they cheered his progress as the flimsy looking two-wheeled sulky in which he rode sped around the smooth dirt oval.

Doc Schoonover had a close kinship with all animals, and nobody was surprised the day he came home carrying a wriggling little black-spotted Dalmatian puppy. From the minute he opened the car door and set the pup on the grass by the driveway, Doc and Ruth Schoonover's place was changed forever.

Popcorn, as they named the little dog, brought with her all the excitement and discovery that comes with any new baby. It didn't take her any time at all to become familiar with her surroundings, and she soon had the run of the farm.

Maybe it was because domestic animals seldom attack or misuse babies of any species, or maybe it was because there really was some love-at-first-sight bond between the pup and the high-spirited horses, but Doc's trotters adopted the puppy almost at once.

Before long, Popcorn was scurrying in and out among the polished hooves of the racehorses, play-nipping at their ankles and yapping with make-believe ferocious warnings and threats. As part of the game, the horses would wrinkle their lips and gently nuzzle the puppy, sometimes actually lifting her off the ground by the scruff of her neck. To her tail-wagging delight, they would shake her gently and set her back upon the ground, unharmed.

Whenever she could get by with it, Popcorn shunned her soft bed on the Schoonovers' back porch to spend the night in the tack room or, on the rare occasions when a stall door was left unlatched, she nosed her way in to curl up next to one of the mares.

She grew from a noisy, tumbling, under-foot puppy to a mature, well-bred "young lady," and the growing companionship between her and the horses was a good thing to see. As summer waned and fall tapered off into winter, it became obvious the Dalmatian had accepted the shepherding and the company-keeping of the horses as her own serious responsibility.

Spring came ultimately to the fields. The ground dried and the grass grew long and sweet, and Doc began letting the horses roam the pasture at night to enjoy the fresh graze and the pleasant weather.

One morning, as he stood at the kitchen window, enjoying his first cup of coffee and counting the faces out at the watering tank, he came up one horse shy of the usual number. He counted again. The familiar white blaze of BiLou, who was due to foal in a couple of days, was definitely not among those fine aristocratic heads clustered near the barnyard gate.

Doc had just about decided that BiLou must have come to early term during the night, when he thought about Popcorn. This would be the first foaling since the dog had come to live at the farm, and he couldn't be sure just what her reaction might be. And, for that matter, he had no idea how BiLou might react to the dog's presence, if Popcorn happened to be there when the mare's foal was born.

Doc raised the kitchen window and whistled for the dog. Immediately there was a scratching outside the kitchen door. As good luck would have it, Popcorn had been penned inside the porch the night before when the back door had unexpectedly swung shut and latched behind her.

Thankful for this turn of events, Doc put down his empty cup and stepped out to the porch. Taking the young dog's muzzle in his hands, he roughed her face and ears, rebuffing her attempts to lick his face, made a couple of well-placed whacks at her hindquarters, and crossed the porch to open the back door.

"Come on, girl; let's go see what's up," he said, and the spotted dog raced ahead of him through the yard, across the gravel drive, and up to the fence. There she stretched tall, her front feet on the gate, greeting her sometime stablemates.

Her accidental capture on the back porch had made Popcorn late for her morning run, so she didn't tarry long with the horses. After their quick greetings, she wriggled through the gate and loped off toward the nearest fence row with its tall grass where rabbits and quail and sometimes a ringneck pheasant might be flushed.

Doc climbed up on the fence to look across the field for his missing mare and saw her standing under the ancient elm in the middle of the pasture. A small red-brown foal was curled at her feet. He quickly stepped down and started across the field, heading toward BiLou, and keeping the dog in sight, off to his right.

Apparently unaware of the newcomer under the elm tree, Popcorn had begun an anxious tail-wagging investigation of the fence row. She had covered the line which extended eastward from the corner of the barn, and turned to cross the end of the field. Suddenly, as she was about even with the big tree, Popcorn stopped in midstride like a setter on point. Body rigid, head high, her nose explored in long, slow breaths the strange scent which was coming to her from the center of the field.

Cautiously, then, she began to move in the direction of BiLou and her foal. Half a dozen yards short of the tree's overhanging branches, Popcorn switched directions and made a big circle around the scene of the foaling, stopping at intervals to raise her head and assay the scene. Each time she stopped to look, she raised her muzzle ever so slightly, then lowered it and moved on.

Popcorn did not approach the mare and foal, but kept her distance and, completing the circle at the point where she had first approached the tree, she again turned eastward and trotted back to the fence row to take up where she had left off her morning hunt. Unmoving, but for a small toss of her head, the mare silently eyed the departing dog.

Doc was puzzled. BiLou had always seemed to be one of Popcorn's favorite mares, and he had expected the dog to show a little more interest in the new foal. At the same time, it was no less than amazing, he mused, that BiLou had so passively endured the dog's approach to her new baby.

What, if anything, he wondered, had passed between BiLou and Popcorn in that brief moment before the dog had turned and trotted away.

The old vet watched the young dog as she reached the end of the fence row and turned west to run along the far East side of the field.

Suddenly, the dog came to a full stop, front feet splayed out ahead of her, ears cocked, skinny tail flag-poling skyward, her head angled to peer into the tall grass. Then she leaped forward and in the same movement, arched her body to toss some small object high over her head, jumping to catch it in her mouth as it fell. She snapped her head sideways two or three times and turned to trot in a beeline toward the elm tree.

Curious, even wary, of what the dog might have in mind, Doc quickened his own steps toward BiLou and her newborn, which would be named Ricann Lou. As before, Popcorn circled the tree a few yards out, until she came abreast of the place where the foal lay. Then, without pause, she turned and walked to the baby horse. The foal raised its red-velvet head to look at the dog.

Then Doc saw what it was Popcorn had brought from the far fence, and he knew he'd never seen anything like this before, nor likely ever would again, as he watched Popcorn gently lay her gift, a small white-bellied field mouse, near the foal's muzzle.

Then, sniffing the baby's small, white-blazed face ever so lightly, Popcorn stretched out upon the ground, her head on her forepaws, and took up vigil over her newest charge.

GIDGET, THE SEAGOING CAT

In its heyday as a fishing center, the little sundrenched village of Madeira Beach, situated about halfway down Florida's west coast, was home to some fifty or so, fair-to-middling-sized workboats which plied their trade in the lucrative waters of the Gulf of Mexico.

An even dozen of these boats, when they were in port, tied up at the weathered docks which skirted the concrete seawall of an establishment known as the Fisherman's Co-op. The boats were called grouper diggers, for their owners earned their bread and butter in long days and nights offshore, hauling the black and the red grouper, those particularly tasty members of the sea bass family, from their ancestral home on the bottom of the Gulf of Mexico.

The Co-op members all knew each other and most of each other's business, for not much happened within the little community which was not talked about on every vessel and in the office of the fishhouse itself.

From time to time, a stray cat or dog would find its way to the Co-op to panhandle a meal and, if one of these travelers happened upon a particularly generous captain, it might hang around for a couple of days, enjoying the largesse. Eventually, though, the call of the road usually won out and the hobo traveled on.

One morning, as the fishermen sat in the Co-op office,

gossiping over their morning coffee, one of the captains mentioned offhandedly that a little black and white cat had just bummed breakfast from his deckhand. That afternoon, word got around that the cat had moved on to take lunch with Jim Payne on the *Madeira Lady*, a grouper digger whose captain was preparing for a trip to sea. Jim had fed the little cat, petted her some, and gone on about his business.

An hour or so later, with his bait and stores and ice all aboard, Jim Payne cast off the lines, yelled goodbye to the fishermen standing around the back door of the fishhouse, and backed *Madeira Lady* out of her slip.

Twenty minutes later, he had passed through the open span of the old cantilever bridge, negotiated the John's Pass channel, and turned, beyond the outer buoy, toward a favorite fishing ground in the Gulf of Mexico.

It was just about then the little black and white cat came curling around his ankles. Realizing he was stuck with her for the eight or ten days he'd be at sea, Jim put down a dish for her and in no time at all, the cat had settled into her chosen role of star boarder. She'd be somebody to talk to when the fish weren't biting, Jim thought.

Much as his liking for the cat grew, however, Jim realized theirs could be only a fleeting relationship; the cat would never be welcome at home. Jim's wife, Margaret, possessed a Siamese who'd already made it clear he wouldn't take kindly to another cat in the house, not even a former stray he might look down his aristocratic nose at and, quite possibly even, boss around some.

Jim needn't have worried about it, however, for the little girl cat had a mind of her own and eight days later, back in port, she jumped ship.

She made the rounds of the fleet, spending a night on first one boat and then another. There were those who said she sat on the dock and sniffed the air at supper time, then chose her night's lodgings by the aroma of a good meal.

A couple of boats up the line from the *Madeira Lady*, Bud Gentry docked *Bearcat*, a sleek 40-footer which had come north from the pompano trade in the Florida Keys. Bud had rigged her out for grouper fishing and renamed her for the last place he'd been assigned in Vietnam.

The little orphan cat, probably a teenager in cat years, was still looking for a home. After her trip on the *Madeira Lady*, she had been free-lancing the fleet for close to a week when Bud stepped aboard one afternoon to find her curled up, asleep, on the starboard bunk.

"That's my bed," he told her; "If you're going to move aboard this boat, you'll have to sleep on the other bunk." Scratching her ears as he picked her up, Bud moved the unresisting cat gently over to the port side.

The cat licked the places where the man had touched her fur, and must have liked the signals the effort gave her about who this person was, for she curled up and was soon fast asleep. When you're in good company, she seemed to say, one bunk is as good as another.

Bud Gentry didn't live aboard *Bearcat* when he was in port. Home, where he and I, our teen-aged son, Ralph, and a Siamese cat named Hannibal lived, was eight or so miles from the beach. But he drove to the boat nearly every day to get fishing reports from the other boat owners and to get equipment and tackle ready for the next trip to sea.

The small cat was still hanging around when he closed up the boat to go home that first evening, so he shooed her out of the cabin, left a bowl of water on deck for her, and told her he'd see her in the morning, if she hadn't moved on.

The next morning, he found her sitting primly on the fish box, amidships, waiting for breakfast.

She licked up every scrap of the meal he put down for her and then, though Bud didn't know it at the time, checked off all the remaining squares on her dance card. Through some means known only to the cat, she had found her fishing partner.

When the day came for Bud to take aboard bait and ice for sea, and I went aboard with fresh linens and a supply of home-cooked goodies for the galley, it didn't take an Einstein to recognize a settled-in cat. I bade her welcome to the family, as well as the boat, added a box of Purina Chow, a litter tray, and a bag of make-believe sand to my shopping list, and struck out for the Ohio Market, over on Gulf Boulevard, to buy supplies.

Later, as I stood on the Kingfisher dock to watch the *Bearcat* through the bridge and out the pass toward open sea, I could see Bud, waving from the pilot house, and his new companion standing high on the console, between the fathometer and the automatic pilot. She stood there in an attitude which said she fully expected to be paid for what she was doing.

Gidget — it was Bud Gentry who named her that — turned out to have a fine set of sealegs and, by the time she'd made her second trip, she'd become a regular, signed-on member of the crew. She soon made it obvious she adored the availability of fresh fish, and early in each trip, Bud would bone and cut up a small grouper and keep the portions on ice for her. When we took her for a checkup and shots, Bill Bone, our veterinarian, warned us about the dangers of feeding a cat too much fish, so Gidget's portions of grouper were doled out as treats between meals of Purina Chow.

During the intervals when Bud was in port, Gidget became, like himself, a temporary landlubber, and she was a fine little houseguest on Lark Drive. She was an industrious small cat and we often mocked the swing of her tiny backside and chanted "plod-plod-plod-plod," as we watched her walk, for she always marched along as though she was late for an appointment or was looking for some job that might need doing.

Even when she watched her favorite TV programs she seemed to have to get involved and sometimes her silhouette, in front of the screen, was almost as entertaining as the people in the show.

Animal movies, particularly westerns, held her undivided attention, as she imitated their action with like movements of her own. I've seen her lean forward until she almost toppled over as she tried to follow the cowboys and their horses over the horizon.

Destined never to be a mother, Gidget proved to be a pretty good foster parent, for while she lived her short but meaningful life with us, we also acquired the baby Barney.

A sealpoint Siamese, Barney was the first store-bought cat I ever had. He came to us creamy white, with just the slightest suggestion of the points which would be his marks of beauty when he grew up. The little slant-eyed kitten was a gift from Bud who made light of the gift, though I knew he was feeling badly about taking Gidget away to sea.

Gidget assumed the responsibility of teaching Barney how to behave in a home where she already held the position of Head Cat. Gidget had taken on a good bit of swagger and sophistication and had undoubtedly earned the right to lord it over any upstart newcomer for, by the time Barney came along, she had made enough trips onto the Gulf of Mexico to trade yarns with the best of ship's cats or any other kind of cat for years to come.

With the arrival of the kitten, I should have put two food bowls down at the end of the kitchen cabinet, but separate diets for kittens hadn't yet become popular so, at feeding time, I just increased the amount of chow in Gidget's bowl. Barney's schooling about who ate first in a two-cat home began immediately.

The slap-happy kitten who, up to this time had never heard the word "no," scampered to Gidget's side and poked his head into the bowl beside hers.

He didn't have time to even blink between that and the half a spilt second later, when Gidget swung at him with her long black arm and slapped him away from the bowl.

Gidget and Barney

Barney lost traction and slid across the waxed kitchen floor, slewed under the bottom shelf of a utility cart, and came to rest against a table leg.

That this treatment was being levied against him deliberately or that he was being denied access to the supper table were the two things farthest from Barney's mind right at that minute, so he shook his head to clear away the smack Gidget had given him and scurried back to where Gidget stood, beside the food bowl.

Gidget smacked him again, and reinforced the lesson with a nasty snarl.

When Barney crawled from under the table the second time, he sat down, where he was, to watch Gidget and try to figure out this business of the smacks and the slides across the kitchen floor. Gidget had already returned to her meal, keeping her near eye on her pupil and, when she was finished, she stalked off into the living room for a bath and a nap.

I picked up Barney and placed him next to the supper dish. He looked over his shoulder toward the living room door through which his self-appointed school marm had disappeared. He was hungry, but he'd begun to get a message about her idea of discipline and wasn't ready to sign up for any more instructions.

Smoothing his fur with a few light strokes of my hand down his back and a sentence or two of sweet nothings in his ear, I placed him next to the bowl, and tipped his nose down to the surface of the chow. "It's okay, Baby. It's okay," I said.

After a moment, the kitten picked up a mouthful of chow, turned to the side, and dropped the food upon the plastic placemat which marked their eating place. Hitching his little rear end around so he could watch the livingroom door, in case Gidget decided to return, he began to eat from the little pile of food.

For the next several days, Gidget would give a low snarl if Barney came near as she ate. Then, she seemed to make up her mind he'd grasped the idea of her seniority, and took him on to the next step in his lessons. When the bowl of food was set out, Gidget walked over to it but ate only a couple of bites. Then she backed away a few steps and sat down.

Barney watched her for several moments, then cautiously went to the bowl, grabbed his usual mouthful, and placed it on the mat. He ate with a wary eye on Gidget, but she didn't interfere.

The routine was established. Gidget had confirmed her right to first bite and, for the rest of her life, the two of them ate in that manner, Barney always eating only after he had carefully removed a mouthful of chow to the floor beside the dish.

Gidget had earned her teacher's license; Barney was an apt pupil.

51

Gidget's industriousness followed her to sea, and it came as no particular surprise to Bud when she began to take on jobs for herself on the boat. The first duty she qualified for, that of weather forecaster, came about as the result of a natural talent.

Bearcat was set up for trips of two weeks' duration and most often, once established on the fishing grounds, Bud and the boat, which was anchored to the bottom of the Gulf of Mexico, fifty to a hundred fathoms below, just rode out whatever weather nature provided. The fishermen called it "hanging on the hook."

Storms were almost always forecast well in advance by the weather bureau. The fishermen learned about them from their radios, and discussed each other's whereabouts, their weather worthiness, and their individual plans to head for shore or ride out the storm, depending upon the progress of a trip and their distance from port, which might easily be a hundred miles — a good day's run.

If an unexpected bit of weather came up during the day, it was usually a gradual thing which a fisherman would notice in time to prepare the decks and gear for a bit of a bounce.

If, on the other hand, a wind came up during the night and caught a lone fisherman sleeping soundly, he might simply be lulled to deeper sleep by the first gentle rocking of the boat and not awaken until a full-fledged blue norther had developed. In that case, gear might suffer damage or even be tossed over the side.

It was in these sneaking-up nighttime storms that Gidget began to pay for her keep. With the keen ability most cats have to sense the first shifts of magnetic or atmospheric forces, Gidget would know of an oncoming storm far in advance of its arrival. When such an awareness came to her at night, she would leave her own bed to climb up and settle down with her chin resting between Bud's knees. There she would brace herself to avoid the tossing about she might otherwise experience on her own bed.

In the process of settling down to ride out the bad weather, Gidget would awaken Bud. Thus alerted in time, he could take steps to protect gear and supplies.

The second duty Gidget volunteered for was a little more complicated and not nearly so accidental.

Into *Bearcat's* deck, aft of the pilot house, had been fitted a set of six specially built and well insulated wood and fiberglass boxes. Before leaving port, some twenty-six hundred pounds of crushed ice would be distributed among five of the boxes. When Bud began to catch fish, he would transfer a bed of ice to the empty box and place a layer of the catch on top of it. In that and successive alternating layers, up to six thousand pounds of fresh fish could be stowed and kept just above the freezing point during the two weeks the trip might last.

From the top of the steering console, the highest point on *Bearcat's* workplace, Gidget daily monitored the work of fishing. She saw the grouper and snapper, averaging twelve to thirty pounds, the smaller but delectable scamp, and the cumbersome warsaw, sometimes weighing over a hundred pounds, when they were brought aboard. And she watched, from her post in the pilot house or from the lid of one of the boxes, as the fish were buried in ice.

Now, far be it from me to presume to guess at what point Gidget decided she needed something to do to fill the long quiet hours of the night. Maybe there was no planning to it; maybe, fresh out of catnaps, she was just out for a nighttime stroll on deck, saw a job which needed doing, and did it.

Bearcat had been in flying fish waters for several days and the pretty little blue creatures had been splashing aboard with unpredictable regularity, to die when they fell on deck. As a part of each morning's chores, Bud would gather up the dead fish and toss them over the side.

Gidget had shown some curiosity about the flying fish at first, but when Bud had offered her one, she decided the firm fleshed, scaly creatures were not nearly as toothsome as the nice grouper fillets she had taught her human to provide.

At any rate, one night Gidget took it upon herself to gather up all of the flying fish which landed upon *Bearcat's* deck while Bud was asleep. There were eight or ten of them, that first night. She carried them down the ladder into the cabin, where she deposited them in a neat pile on the floor, beside her fishing partner's bunk. When Bud awoke in the morning and swung his bare feet toward the floor, he found them.

Turning on the lamp over his bunk, he saw Gidget, seated in the galley, which was located catty-corner across the way, watching him. Later, he would swear she wore a satisfied grin.

"Gidget," he said, "you can't bring those fish in here," and from where he sat, he began pitching them, one by one, through the cabin door, onto the deck outside.

Gidget might have been at the net line of an important tennis match, as she followed the progress of each of the fish flashing past her. After all of her carefully gathered catch had disappeared out the cabin door, she continued to sit, with what Bud called a frown on her face while he put coffee on to perk and went into the head for his morning shave.

When he came back into the cabin, the first thing he noticed was the neat pile of flying fish, lying again beside his bunk. Gidget's long front legs had never been more rigid; her half-folded ears had a purposeful look about them; the tiny movement in the curled tip of her tail underscored a look of defiance as she glowered from her seat in the galley.

"Now, Gidget, you can't bring these in here," he said, and he picked up a handful, climbed through the hatch, and tossed them over the side. Gidget, he noticed, had a set to her brow which might have been taken for an uncertainty about resigning this ship's papers when her current enlistment ran out.

On the following night, another supply of flying fish ended their brief spurt of airborne energy over *Bearcat's* deck and fell there. Once again, Gidget gathered them up and carried them down the ladder, into the cabin. And again, Bud found them beside his bunk when he awoke, just before daylight. Their disposal was a repeat of the previous morning's drill, with Gidget, again, obviously upset over his lack of gratitude for her work.

It may seem that it would have been a small thing for Bud to have played Gidget's game. He might have made a proper fuss over the fish for her sake and then disposed of them while she was off on one of her walks around the deck, or when she went to the forepeak to watch the dolphins playing in the bow wave.

Much as he liked the little cat, he might have done that, except that there were lots of places on *Bearcat* where Gidget might have taken a small fish, but where Bud couldn't reach. He knew, for instance, that if Gidget ever decided to take one of her prizes into the cat-size space next to the hull, behind fuel or water tanks, the cabin would be pretty nigh unliveable by the time he'd returned to port and torn out the tanks to get to it.

For this reason, he knew he must put a stop to Gidget's night shift activities. That evening, and on succeeding nights, he put the bugscreen in place at the top of the ladder, so the cat couldn't go in and out.

Gidget put on a pout which lasted at least until lights out and Bud had no idea how long after, and several trips would be completed before Gidget finally accepted the edict that she was not to bring fish into the cabin.

Gidget continued to serve as boat cat until *Bearcat* was sold; then, cat and captain came permanently ashore. That summer she traveled with us to northern British Columbia, where, in a new role as camp cat, she was a ray of sunshine to the members of a crew searching, more or less unsuccessfully, for gold.

One night, several happy, healthy years later, when Barney had reached the age of two or three years, he and Gidget were playing a simple ambush and tackle game which they often enjoyed. Suddenly, for no apparent reason, Gidget collapsed in a heap, panting heavily.

When she did not recover within a half hour, I called Bill Bone. He advised me to watch her closely, to offer her nothing more than water until morning, and then to give him a call.

The next morning, when I told him her condition was no better, he said to bring her in right away. After his examination, I left her for tests and went home alone, taking with me only that sinking feeling I always have when I must leave a beloved pet in hospital.

Early the next day, when the test results were complete, Bill called to say he needed to do surgery; that she had a ruptured diaphragm, a condition which had probably been waiting to happen for most of her life. He said he couldn't guarantee results, but without an operation to try to correct her problem, she would simply die after suffering a great deal of pain.

I explained the situation to Bud and a far-away look fell upon his face as he remembered a time when Gidget had

56

patiently endured a thing every blue-water sailor dreads.

On a night when the seas and the wind had risen to gigantic proportions and *Bearcat* was riding waves whose height were as much as her own length, Bud and Gidget, as usual, braced themselves as best they could and slept.

During the night, they were jolted awake when the boat fell off a 40-footer she had ridden to its crest. Every hatch slammed open, from the rope bin to the cabin skylight. With the suddenness of a sneeze, Bud, Gidget, and everything in the cabin were drenched with enough saltwater to have floated the lifeboat which was strapped to the cabin roof.

As automatic pumps took over to empty the water back over the side, Bud grabbed dry towels from the galley to mop up his sleeping space and dry himself off. Gidget righted herself and hopped upon the fresh towel he placed in a corner of her quickly stripped down bunk.

There she patiently licked the saltwater from her black and white fur, showing none of the righteous indignation she had displayed over the loss of a few flying fish on an earlier occasion.

Now, remembering how the little black and white cat had filled the lonely hours at sea, Bud didn't take long to decide about the possibility of surgery. "Tell him to do it," he said.

Using the most sophisticated life-support equipment available for animals, Bill Bone tried to save Gidget's life but, as an anesthetic was being administered before the surgery, the spunky little cat's labored breathing stopped.

With all her boundless energy, she simply had not been able to outrun the only predator she had ever encountered.

SWAN SONG

An ad clerk named Judy took the first call informing the Seminole Beacon, a local weekly newspaper, about the disappearance of a pet swan. Right away, Judy sensed there might be a story in it. The editor agreed and, that week, the paper carried a picture of the two swans, serenely afloat in their private paradise, with the caption:

"Mike and Ike, in happier days, before the disappearance of Mike (on the left)."

The accompanying article asked whether anyone had seen Mike, a beautiful, long-necked swan, last seen in the pond behind his owners' home. His identical twin, Ike, the article said, was suffering great depression. He no longer frolicked under the water fountain; he wouldn't eat; he wasn't doing any of the things which had become normal activity for the brother swans over the past eight years.

It was believed by the owners, Anne and Bob Lonardo, as well as the police — they had been called but could find neither bill nor feather of the missing bird — that someone had lured Mike away.

Mike, the Lonardos agreed, was the more aggressive of

the pair, and would certainly have protested if parties unknown had attempted to heist him. However, no sign of shed feathers, which would have been lost in such a struggle, had been found.

There had been a glitch in the electronic lock on the Lonardo estate's large double gate, the article went on, and the owners guessed that perhaps the disappearance had occurred while the gate was out of order. A telephone number appeared in the article and a reward was offered for information about the swan-napper.

The following week, the Beacon reported that Mike had not been found and that, after the electronic gate had been repaired, Mike's pond mate, Ike, was missing.

The Lonardos, the second article claimed, were heartbroken. They couldn't imagine anyone's stealing the swans, but it was openly conjectured that a plot to steal must, indeed, have been carried out.

"While the swan-nappers may not be armed and dangerous," ran the article, "knowing the Lonardos' sadness leads us to believe the criminals have hearts of ice."

Again, there was a plea for information, this time with the assurance of anonymity for the informant. The offer of a reward was repeated and Mrs. Lonardo was quoted as having said that if some young prankster was the culprit, she would happily buy the youngster a swan of his or her own. Plus food. *If she got her swans back.*

The third week, in Letters to the Editor, an item appeared chiding the cold-hearted members of the press for having allowed a love story to slip past them. The writer theorized the swans had reached adulthood and answered the mating call. He offered, parenthetically, the information that bald eagles begin mating after three years of age.

The writer further pointed out that the swans might not

59

return after mating because they mate for life and only if their respective mates agree, might they return home!

The writer did not reveal the source of these revelations concerning the romantic attachments of swans, but he challenged the editor to seek authentication of his opinions from the local Audubon Society and to print the story to let him know he was right.

As for myself, concerned with other matters, I did not read these articles thoroughly at the time. I would remember, later, however, having seen the swans' photograph in the newspaper. And, still later, I would be moved to sort through a stack of old newspapers to dig out the items which had chronicled their disappearance.

Now, it was the end of the third week of the mystery. I can't recall exactly what it was that had made that Friday such a bad day, but by five o'clock I was ready to shut down the corner where I write, dig out a box of ice cream and a long handled spoon, and crawl off somewhere with some light reading.

At any rate, I wasn't all that happy about answering the telephone when it rang, and even less willing to get excited about the caller who said her swans were penned up under a neighbor's porch and she was afraid to go in after them; they might get mean.

I wasn't sure if she meant the swans or the neighbors, but she cleared that up. She said that Mike, one of the swans, was inclined, at times, to be somewhat of a rouser.

My caller, as she told the story for the second time, identified herself as the lady with the missing swans — the lady from the newspaper article. She said she was sorry if she sounded excited, but a policeman had found the missing birds, right in her neighborhood. The pair had wandered into her yard, the neighbor had said, and it was certainly okay for the owner to have them back.

The policeman, however, didn't want anything to do with capturing them. The officer of the law reported that one of the birds seemed to be injured. Its wing, he said, was all trussed up with silver duct tape. He had heard how a wounded animal might turn on a person trying to rescue it.

My caller said she couldn't see how her swans had gotten away in the first place, over an eight-foot concrete wall.

"Could there be a hole in the wall?" I asked.

"Absolutely not," answered my informant.

The swans had been gone for three weeks, she went on to say, and if we didn't get them back today, we would be into another weekend and everyone knows we can't get anything done on a weekend. She said she'd called the big newspapers and the county agent, the sheriff, animal rescue, and the seabird sanctuary, and each of them seemed to think the situation was out of their jurisdiction.

"Why me?" I asked. She said the Beacon had told her I was interested in birds and animals and might be able to help.

For emphasis, I suppose, she went through the whole thing again. As I listened, I was thinking there wasn't much I could do about a pair of swans, especially when one of them was inclined, on occasion, to get mean. I often drop what I'm doing to rescue wild birds in distress, but I'm not all that keen about interfering in domestic problems, avian or otherwise. Then, something in the lady's voice made me weaken, and I heard myself promising I'd at least go with her to the neighbor's yard, to have a look at her swans, if she was sure the neighbor wasn't going to object. She said again that the neighbor was kindly disposed, having indicated the swans had just wandered into the yard and she'd penned them for safekeeping, since she didn't know who they belonged to.

I didn't quite understand the logic of that, but figured

that's what happens when neighbors hide themselves from each other behind eight-foot concrete walls. If I was going to be involved, I decided, I'd leave the chatting between the neighbors to the neighbors and just work with the facts I had. I told Mrs Leonardo that, if I drove over and had a look, maybe I'd be able to suggest a way of coaxing them out from under the porch and back to their own yard.

Twenty minutes later, I had driven across town and located the Lonardo's estate, which sprawls along the shore of Florida's Gulf Intercoastal Waterway. I introduced myself to Anne and Bob Lonardo, and post haste, Anne and I were in a golf cart, whirring down the long, paved driveway, up the street, and back an equally long driveway, to find ourselves far beyond the tall ivy-covered wall which squares off the Lonardo estate.

Anne — we were using first names by now — was still rattling on, asking me to tell her just why those swans would want to leave home in the first place, with a beautiful spring-fed pond and their own shower bath and an endless supply of horse pellets to eat and, besides, they each had a clipped wing, so they couldn't fly over the wall even if they wanted to; they'd have had to come out the gate or swim away, and the Intracoastal Waterway is saltwater and they surely wouldn't like that.

I interrupted her to say, "Are those your swans?"

Anne looked where I was pointing, and said, "Oh, my gawd. My poor babies."

The problem was, she hadn't recognized her own birds and had steered the golf cart right past the tall wire enclosure which penned them into a corner, under the porch.

As a matter of fact, it wasn't under exactly what I'd call a porch, but more like the run-around balcony of a second story. I'd imagined shinnying under the floor of a first-story porch, feeling around in the dark for a couple of angry, big-beaked birds. What I saw now might make the task just a tad easier.

It was no wonder Anne Lonardo hadn't recognized Mike and Ike, for instead of the glistening white, proud, tall swans which had been pictured in the Seminole Beacon, here was a pair of gray-dirty, waddling-in-dust birds with some indescribable quality about them I couldn't put a name to. Later, when I heard Anne trying to say how awful they looked, the words came to me. "They'd been stripped of their dignity," I said, and I had to make up the other word which helped describe the swans: "They were humilified."

Well, when I saw the fix those birds were in, I just lost any idea I might have had about simply making suggestions, and said, "I'll give it a try."

I ran a quick trial scenario for the swans' rescue through my mind. I carry a long-handled dip net in the trunk of the Taurus for the general run of bird rescues I get called out on, but I didn't think that would do the trick in this case; Mike and Ike were two pretty big birds. "Let's go get a bedsheet," I said.

Anne turned the key, the golf cart hummed to life, and we hurried back to the Lonardo estate. She took the elevator to the second floor and returned almost immediately with a king size sheet balled up under her arm. Her husband, Bob, was with her.

Bob Lonardo, who uses the golf cart to get around the property due to polio he had when he was a child, decided he'd join us in our rescue mission.

Suddenly elevated from suggestion-maker to the status of an expert called in to take care of a difficult problem, for Anne and Bob seemed to have no doubt I would do just that, I climbed into the front of the golf cart with Bob while Anne rode, shotgun style, on the back.

Off we whirred, down the driveway, along the street, and back out to the home of the Lonardos' next door neighbor who, after a half-welcoming wave from the second floor balcony, disappeared inside.

The home was a two-story cedar stilt house, with the living quarters above first story, as local building codes require now on waterfront property. Along one side, an open stairway rose to a balcony porch, which surrounded the home's second floor. The area under the steps and the balcony had been enclosed with wire fencing and it was in this narrow, dirt-floored pen that the once-elegant swans now stood: desolate, dirty, forlorn, unable to escape.

Their only access to water was a half-filled tin can, wired to a post at what, to them, was chest level. Nowhere was there any sign of the sort of body of water a swan needs for feeding and drinking — a pool, pond, or shallow lake, where it may swim to feed from the bottom and drink by plunging its head and neck under the surface. Again the Lonardos cautioned me that Mike was inclined to be feisty in even the best of times and had been known to attack if his space was threatened.

I realized that anywhere I went in that smallish pen, I would be threatening Mike's space. Now, however, as I studied the swans to decide upon a plan for their rescue, they seemed subdued, to say the least. At any rate, I decided to attack the problem without further delay and entered the pen, carrying the sheet over my arm.

Walking cautiously, herding the two big birds ahead of me, I worked my way around the first turn and toward the end of the pen. About midway down the long side of the house, Mike spooked and turned back, so I let him drift back past me and, with the sheet spread out bull fighter fashion, I moved

Ike into a corner.

Crouching over the frightened, wounded swan, and talking to him in the softest of sweet-baby tones, I moved my right hand slowly up his long neck and grasped his heavy bill. Dropping to my knees, I reached under Ike with my left hand to seize a leg, just above its powerful gray foot. Edging down, with my right elbow, I pushed the right leg into reach of my left hand and grabbed it, too. Using my elbows and chin and feet, I worked the sheet, which I'd never let go of, closely around the big bird. Then, I struggled to my feet and carried him back to where the Lonardos greeted me with cheers.

Sitting on the front seat of the golf cart, I leaned over to hold the swan on the floor at my feet while Bob drove quickly to the pond in the Lonardo's back yard. There, I set Ike free upon the ground and unwound the sheet. It was only moments before he realized where he was. He faced the pond, fell to his belly, and slid into the water. Back in his proper element, he paddled immediately to the center of the pond.

He made it seem like he was awfully glad to get away from people.

Mike's capture wasn't really anything more than a repeat of Ike's, but the "rescue" took place around the corner, out of their sight, and the Lonardo's didn't see how easy it really was. Remembering their caution about Mike's sometimes becoming ill-tempered, and especially remembering that the local police had not felt up to the task, I just let them go ahead and cheer when they saw me walk around the corner with Mike in my arms. When they said I was a brave, spunky little lady, I didn't see any reason to argue.

The real show came when we were back on the Lonardo's property, approaching the pretty little body of water which was home to the brother swans. Ike heard the golf cart whispering across the grass and left the center of the pond to swim toward us.

As soon as Mike's feet were on the ground and he was free of the king size sheet, he, too, bellied down and slid into the water, hurrying to Ike's side.

Just like that, back together and where they belonged, those swans took back their dignity, despite being dirty, and Ike still wore the ugly frayed strips of silver gray tape on his wing.

There in the pond they met and, with every ounce of their inherited nobility, they touched cheeks with the barest contact, making a picture-perfect heart shape of their curving necks and sleek heads. Then, perfectly choreographed, their sinuous necks swooped downward in unison, and they drank deeply, their heads submerged.

They were home, and the Lonardos were so happy about the way things turned out they no longer even cared how or why the swans had left home in the first place.

Getting the tape off Ike's wing would come later. Getting Don Howell, my vet, over to check them out, would come later, too. And, between them, Mike and Ike would forever guard the secret of their disappearance.

As for me, it was enough just to see the brother swans' joy in being afloat together, after three weeks in that dry-dirt pen.

I didn't hang around. The celebration, which began as I was leaving, was too much of a family thing.

LOST AND FOUND

Jasper

It was a cold and rainy day when the yellow tiger kitten made his way to the back door of the comfortable home where Frank and Ollie lived. There the poor little cat sat, dripping and bedraggled, until Ollie heard his cries and went to investigate. "You poor little boy," she cooed, as she carried him inside.

Sensing that he'd stumbled upon decidedly better times than experience had led him to expect, he endured a brisk rubdown with a soft, warm towel, then made short work of a saucer of milk. Before long, he lay curled upon the hearth, near the blazing fire, where he slept away the memory of his beginnings, as well as the forever unsolved mystery of the misfortune which had cast him to the fates on so miserable a day.

His fur, when dry, had the same dusty yellow tones of the small piece of semi-precious jasper Ollie had collected on a trip through the west, and from this, she gave him his name.

Jasper was soon ordering the routine of the two people who lived in the red brick house on Cherry Lane. They gave him regular brushings, saw to it that he ate only those foods which pleased him most, and they provided him with private facilities so he would never again have to go outside in rain or cold.

Before long, they learned that, when the weather was fine, he liked to be outside, his collar fastened to a line attached reassuringly to the back door. There he could nap cozily when sun warmed the patio, or make quiet-as-breath threats against the squirrels which scampered, just out of reach, in the oak shaded yard.

Resolutely putting his own taken-in status out of mind, he disallowed the infringement of his territory by any other animal and made short work of saying so. Always in a quiet voice, however, for he had quickly learned that a loud voice brought an unpleasant reaction, while a tiny, timid manner of speaking had the twofold advantage of being ever so much less bothersome to execute, and brought oohs and aahs of admiration from those who heard it. As a result, he was soon completely out of the habit of speaking loudly.

When the Florida cat came for a visit, Jasper would listen to none of her tales of adventure, even though she had exciting stories to tell of her own losing and finding, and of her eventual employment as ship's cat on a very fine and prosperous fishing vessel.

Instead, with nasty, albeit softly spoken, language he made certain she spent the greater part of her visit scrunched uncomfortably under the bed in her own people's room. He forbid her to leave traces of her own scent about his water dish, and he made it plain she would have to get someone to provide her own litter box.

It was only as the Florida cat's stay was coming to an end that his undeniable curiosity about her got the better of him.

Quite early on the day scheduled for her departure, Jasper managed to quietly paw at the bedroom door so that she would find it open and he hoped, make her way into the parlor and onto the seat of the broad bay window, a place in the morning sun which any feline with an ounce of sense would be unable to resist.

It wasn't long before he found her there, preening and yawning and allowing his sunbeam to light upon her glossy black fur in a thoroughly enchanting way. It was almost enough to make him wish he'd made her acquaintance sooner, but he reasoned that any cat who would stay under a bed for hours at a time and who had been content with the very narrowest of windowsills for out-looking, probably wasn't very interesting anyhow.

So later that same day, the sleek and beautiful Gidget — he had to admit, finally, that she was sleek and beautiful — went out of his life as she had come into it — a casual visitor, uninvited, and soon like his own past, forgotten.

Jasper lived in pampered comfort for many years. His cherished Ollie showed her adoration for him in ways which kept him comfortably well fed and allowed him to enjoy a serene existence, free of rude handling by small people and the unpleasant attentions of strangers. Ollie finally managed to understand that it was her black Persian lamb coat that he most especially coveted to lie upon for afternoon naps, and consented to make it available to him on very special occasions.

Frank always managed to cut Jasper's calf liver treats just so and to place only perfectly ripened portions of canteloupe, his favorite treat, upon Jasper's luncheon plate.

Jasper responded to all of these special attentions with just the correct display of affection to ensure that nothing would ever be allowed to change.

True enough, sometimes Ollie held him so tightly that he came near protesting but, remembering in time the warmth of the Persian lamb coat and the delightful taste of out-of-season canteloupe, he always thought better of the momentary discomfort and simply endured such overpowering evidence of her affection.

And then, one morning, Ollie was not there to gather him into her ample lap, to coo soft words into his fur, and to hug him. There were strangers in the house for days, and Frank even forgot about Jasper's daily brushing. When the strangers left, the house seemed empty.

Ollie didn't come back.

Frank shuffled quietly about the big house, ate irregular meals and, in general, neglected many of the routine events Jasper had come to expect. The door to the large front parlor was often closed, denying him access to the sunshine which warmed the cushions in the bay window. The Persian lamb coat was always available now, on what had once been Ollie's bed, but before long it lost the comforting scent of her which had lingered there before. It was less inviting, anyhow, since she was not there to brush away the yellow fur which collected upon it.

The once busy house no longer contained the exciting aromas of cooking or the adventure of just-brought-in packages to be sniffed and investigated. Life became an ever narrowing existence. Whole rooms went unused. Broken things were not repaired; used things were not put away; and Jasper became hard put to find places to curl up where he had not already left an uncomfortable layer of shed fur. Even the lady who came to clean seemed disinclined to entertain him as she once had.

If it hadn't been for the attention he got from his daily combing and the treats of cut-up fresh liver and canteloupe, it would have been a bleak existence, indeed.

Such was the state of affairs when, in the middle of a quiet day, Frank called me on the telephone. He was obviously upset and, from the sound of his voice, he was close to tears, a thing I had seen rarely from him in my lifetime.

"What's wrong, Daddy?" I asked.

"Jasper's gone," he said, choking on the words.

"He's gone?" I asked. "What happened?"

"He must have got out when I went out to the garage last night. He's just not here. I've looked everywhere I could think of, and I been to the neighbors, and nobody's seen him. I went to the paper and put in an ad and said I'd give a hundred dollars to have him back. He's just not here, and I've got no place else to look."

In the days which followed, I talked to Daddy almost daily. He refused to be cheered out of the great loss of the cat which had been his only constant companion since Ollie's death.

I talked with Mrs. Fisher, the lady who came in on Thursdays to put the house in order. Always careful not to upset any of Daddy's cherished routines, she never bothered the collection of favorite magazines piled by his chair, and she never put away the clean underwear which he preferred to leave stacked handily on the clothes drier near his bathroom door. In his present sad state, she said, she tried to keep his quiet life undisturbed. She reported that he walked about the neighborhood daily, still looking for some trace of the missing yellow cat.

During the week which followed, the advertisement in *The Courier* was renewed and neighbors were reminded, almost daily, to keep an eye out for Jasper. Nearly everyone who knew Daddy heard of the cat's disappearance. He reasoned that no one who lived within the town's broad boundaries was so far away that the cat might not have made his way to them. Well-meaning friends suggested he get another cat, but Daddy was determined that none could take Jasper's place.

71

Jasper had been missing for a full two weeks when Daddy called early one morning, and I heard laughter in his voice for the first time since the cat's disappearance. Obviously excited, he shouted, "You'll never guess where I found old Jasper!"

"No, Daddy; where?" I replied, picking up on his excitement.

"In my underwear drawer! He'd been there all along. I went to get out some summer undershirts, and there he was. He just blinked his eyes and came right out."

"Well, Daddy, didn't he ever meow, for you to let him out?" I asked, scarcely able to believe what he was telling me. "Is he terribly thin? Is he all right?"

"Sure he's all right," Daddy bubbled. "There wasn't anything wrong with him, except he was awful thirsty. He drank a whole bowlful of water and I filled it up again, and he drank that too. Mrs. Fisher said she thought she heard him once, when she went in the bedroom to clean, but then she didn't hear it any more. She had the vacuum cleaner running. You know, Jasper's got such a tiny voice."

Now, the grief of the past two weeks behind him, Daddy could laugh at the whole improbable incident, as well as at himself. "I guess I'll have to start putting my clean underwear away when I take them out of the drier," he said, and hung up the telephone to go cut up some fresh calf liver for Jasper.

*   *   *   *   *

Murka

The train traveling southward through the dark and frozen Russian countryside lurched unexpectedly. In the cramped space of the basket which she occupied beneath her master's

72

seat, Murka awoke with a start, mewed softly, and curled her long flag of a tail more closely about her.

Murka's tortoiseshell fur was covered with dry, evil-tasting coal dust which sifted from the stove at the far end of the jostling railroad car. She was in need of a bath and she was cold, for the stove warmed only those nearest its heat. She was hungry; when hot tea had been served to the passengers, no one had thought to bring a saucer of milk to Murka.

Soon after the train had left Moscow, she had begun to cry loudly, but her cries had gone unanswered. Now, she mewed only faintly and only occasionally.

The cat had lost all understanding of why she had been whisked away from her home in Moscow. She remembered neither the scolding nor the sounds made by her weeping mistress, pleading with the master, who now accompanied Murka on her journey.

The truth was that, in the middle of a winter night, Murka had awakened hungry, and she had misbehaved terribly. In the morning, when the family arose from their night's sleep, it was discovered her owners' two pet canaries were missing and Murka was not crying for breakfast as she usually did.

Murka would have to be punished, and it was decided she must go to live with her people's relatives in Voronezh, on the River Don, over 450 train miles southeast of the Russian capital.

And so, this long, dark, train ride.

When the journey ended, she was taken into the home of strangers, in a strange city. At last she had been well-fed and, after giving herself a bath, she curled up on a warm rug and slept.

When she awoke, her master was gone. She looked for him throughout the house, but he was nowhere to be found.

The last trace of him ended at the door and there, feeling lonely and deserted, she cried aloud.

Her cries were mistaken for a polite request to go outside, and the door was opened. Happy to be free from the strange people, the strange smells, and the loneliness, Murka ran into the night.

Before long, her family in Moscow received a letter from the relatives in Voronezh, telling them that Murka had disappeared. Again, her mistress cried, but the master said, "It's probably just as well."

Nearly a year had passed when a catcry was heard in the stairwell of her Moscow family's small apartment and the mistress of the house went to investigate.

At the bottom of the stairs, looking upward, stood Murka. When she heard their excited cries of welcome, she bounded up the stairs and her forgiving mistress knelt to take the weary cat into her arms.

There was a completely healed nick on Murka's left ear; her black and gold fur had grown to cover the place where the tip of her tail had vanished during her absence. The pads of her feet were scarred and swollen. Those bits of evidence were all her family would ever learn of the trials she had known during her absence and the journey she had made to return to the family she loved.

Her old familiar food dish was hastily retrieved from the back of a shelf and the cat ate ravenously everything they placed in it.

Then, curled upon her favorite rug, a contented Murka slept for three days.

BUSTER

Buster

Like the fire itself, the rowdiness around the circle had died down. Sparks no longer rode upward on smoke curls to explode against the sky. The boys' parents, well-fed, for the most part, had left for home better'n an hour ago and the boys, flushed with praise, had cleaned up the mess they'd made cooking supper. Now, as they settled down, their faces reflected the glow of the lowering flames.

At the top of the circle, Scoutmaster Fred Jahns sat Indian fashion with his knees crossed and his heels tucked under his thighs.

"You boys did a good job tonight," Fred said. "I think your folks found out you can make some pretty fine meals, using nothing but a campfire, hot rocks, and a few pieces of wrinkle tin roofing. I was proud of you." Turning to one side, he said, "We got any more firewood over there, Buck?"

Twelve-year-old Lyle Delhotal, the boy everyone called Buck, got up to look. "Got one more pine knot," he answered.

"Well, throw it on the fire, and when it burns down, we'll call it a night," said their leader.

75

Buck placed the piece of wood at the edge of the fire and toed it over to the center of the coals, where, directly, it caught and began to snap and sizzle.

Almost every boy had something to say about what his mom or dad, or somebody else's mom or dad, had had to say about their supper. Mostly, it was good remarks they repeated.

Eventually, though, they ran out of supper talk and their conversation turned to the subject of bad guys. Lee Center, Illinois, where they all lived, lay smack in the middle of what was once known as banditi country and its history furnished plenty for boys to mull over on a dark night.

They'd all been to the big cave dug out under the barn on the old Bliss place, east of town, but the tunnel from the barn to the river hadn't been passable during the lifetime of any of them. Having never seen the tunnel, though, didn't keep a bunch of boys from describing it, down to a tee, or from speculating how many bandits had got away through the tunnel and how many others had been gunned down trying to make it to the river.

Truth to tell, the Lee Center boys were all kind of proud of just how evil their town had once been, back at the time when most of their grandfathers were just boys.

"My dad says Lee Center was too goldarn lawless to be made the county seat, so Judge Dixon give 'um that piece of high ground where the court house sets," one boy volunteered. "It was prob'ly clear out in the country then, with no town a-tall around it."

"Yeah," said another, "and they built a town and named it after him. Dixon."

Bud Gentry had heard most of the stories from his grandpa, John Gentry. Now, Bud spoke up. "Grandpa says Lee Center was as big as Chicago in those days, 'cause

Chicago hadn't started growing yet. These days, he says, y'd prob'ly have to include my dog and his and maybe a few more, just to count four hundred souls in Lee Center."

Boney Welman had pulled a wax paper pack of crumbly crackers out of his pocket and, as he chewed a handful of the crumbs, sputtering some, he told about the skeleton somebody claimed to have found in the old stone quarry, maybe as recently as when his daddy had been a boy. Still had six-guns and holsters strapped on, they said.

"That ain't nothin'; my dad says they's a fella out at the cemetery that was nominated to run for president of the United States, and he ain't even buried under the ground. He's just layin there in a up-ground crypt with a glass top on his casket; him, and his wife, and a little baby, all got glass topped caskets. Dad says they used to let people go in the crypt on the Fourth of July and see their faces through the glass." It was Bud's cousin, Jim Gentry, who contributed those facts.

The last piece of firewood had flared briefly and begun to die down. Now, darkness was moving in on them from the woods. They could still see one another's sunburned faces shining but, beyond that, everything was blanked out by the night. The air had cooled off some and, one by one, they hunched just a little bit closer to the dying fire.

"You s'pose we could git in there to see them dead people?" somebody asked.

"Nah," answered Bud, with the voice of authority. "I and Whitey been down there and looked, and it's locked up solid and the hinges is all rusted over. We saw the man's name on a plate on the door, though; it's George Haskel. If ol' George's own ghost wanted outa there, it couldn't git past them rusty hinges."

"I ain't goin' in no cemetery to look at no dead person,"

said Jimmy. "You kin just count me out."

"Scared a ghost'll git ya?" queried Bud, who wasn't scared of much of anything, and liked to take potshots at his cousin.

"No, I ain't a-scared. I just wouldn't wanna do it, that's all," answered Jim.

There was a rustling noise off in the woods, just then, and it suddenly got so quiet you could have heard an acorn hit the ground a half a mile away. Faces froze stiff and nothing moved but eyeballs as each one of the boys looked around the circle to see how everyone else was reacting to the noise.

Nobody had started breathing yet when the night was suddenly split apart by a terrible sound.

It began with a screech like rusty metal on rusty metal, and there wasn't a boy there didn't look over at Bud Gentry, thinking about what he'd said about George Haskel's ghost maybe wanting to get out past those rusty hinges.

After the screech, the sound rose an octave or so, wavering as it climbed. It fluttered there in mid-air, kind of caught a breath, and slid back down the scale like a lost and dying soul. It made a long drawn-out snork sound, like you do when you forgot your handkerchief and need one real bad. And then, the sound quit.

Still, nobody moved.

Except Fred Jahns, who happened to be sitting with his back to the noise.

Without any help from his hands, and without first unfolding his knees or even bringing his heels out from under him, the boy scout leader just rose straight up - him and the hair on his head at the same time. Eyebrows, too. As he rose up, he let out a great big gush of air that was somewhere between a snore and a yell. Somebody said afterward that maybe that big gush of air was the first thing that happened and it just pulled Fred up with it. That would account for the

78

fact it had all looked so easy.

Then all around the circle there was the combined gasp of all the boys, and it was like on each one of their faces, their own personal gasp blew their eyes wide open, just like Fred's gasp had pulled him off the ground.

And then they all just kind of stiffened and sat there, looking from one to the other.

Except for Bud Gentry. Directly, Bud broke into a big grin and stood up and said, "Hey, you guys, that ain't nothing but ol' Buster. He ain't nothing to be scared of." Bud rummaged in his backpack, found an apple, and loped off in the direction the sound had come from.

Pretty soon, the boys could hear Bud talking low, but they couldn't tell what he was saying till he raised his voice and hollered, "You guys can come on over; it's jist ol' Buster."

There was a little rusty squeak, off to one side, as Fred Jahns' opened his lantern to light it with a kitchen match, and another squeak as he lowered the glass globe over the burning wick. The light glowed and reached out in a circle around Fred as he walked toward the sound of Bud's voice. The boys followed, keeping close to Fred and the light.

Bud was reaching over a wire fence, feeding the apple to the ugliest horse any of them had ever encountered.

Everything they could see about that horse was drooping, from its ears and the bags under its eyes to its cheeks and lips, and the ropes of dried out muscle in its neck. Its eyelids sagged and made it look like it was almost asleep as it slobbered and chewed on the apple.

"This here's Buster," Bud said, and he sounded like he was kind of proud to know the ugly old horse. "He belongs to Mister Joe Graff, and I git to ride him out to bring in the cows when I'm workin' hand for Mister Graff."

"Was that him made that noise?" asked the Kalstead boy.

"Yeah." Bud Gentry was beginning to feel the importance of being the only one who could answer questions about the old bony horse. "He can't help that. He's got something bad wrong with his throat and that's the best he can do for a whinny. He likely heard us over here and just come over to be around people."

Buster had finished the apple and was reaching toward the other boys, making passes at them, flapping his rubbery lips, and showing what few long, yellow teeth he had left. Some of the other boys brought apples from their packs and, at first, Buster ate everything he was offered. He finally had his fill, though, and after a couple of smelly belches, he turned to wander away from the fence, out of the circle of the lantern's light.

As the horse turned, the boys could tell he'd probably been an awful big, powerful horse in his day, but now you could see the individual bones in his spine sticking straight up, with the rest of his body matching the front of him, bone for bone and sag for sag.

For awhile, they tried to coax the horse back, till Bud told them it was no use; Buster had had enough. By ones and twos they made their way back to the almost dead fire and, pretty soon, they all settled down into their quilts and sleeping bags.

It wasn't long before total darkness, and then total quiet, and then a light dew settled down over Fred Jahns and the Lee Center boy scout troup.

* * * * *

It may have been later that same summer; it may have been another summer, but it was getting on toward the middle of August when the argument over horses came up among the

80

regulars in Russel Gentry's tavern.

Russel, Bud's dad, had started his business as a hole-in-the-wall garage and, for awhile, it did pretty well. When an old car broke down and its owner couldn't afford to trade up, Russ would take the car in, work it over, and get it back out on the road. But pay was slow coming in, and the needs of a family of six were hardly being met at all, so sometime, along about the spring of 1939, Russel had made some changes.

After working on cars every day till the middle of the afternoon, he'd close up the garage and go home to an early supper. His wife, Jesse, with the help of the two older boys, Bud and Kay, grew a big garden and fattened a couple of pigs and a beef steer every summer. Jesse was a good cook and always had a hot meal waiting when Russel hurried in from the garage.

After his meal, he'd hustle on back to the garage, where he'd shift things around, over to one side, and unlock the bar supplies. Setting out a row of wooden stools next to a wide shelf, he'd open the outside door which led to the bar side of the building. Just that easy, he was in the tavern business, from then until everyone went home and the sidewalks automatically rolled up, around ten-thirty.

From the first day it was open, Gentry's Tavern became a gathering place for the farmers who would stop by, on their way home from town, for a cold bottle of Schlitz and maybe a nickel bag of Planter's peanuts or one of Jesse's pickled eggs. Gradually, the clientele expanded to include some of the town people. Everybody knew everybody else; there weren't any secrets in the small town, for it was well recognized that men were every bit as efficient as the women at trading information about the people they knew.

On the day in question, Joe Graff had come into town to

81

settle up for a wagonload of oats he'd sold at the grain elevator. He was sitting at the bar, finishing off his second beer, when Andy Delhotal came through the door.

Anybody could tell right off there was a big difference in these two men. Joe Graff, medium to short in height and built like a wrestler, was a good farmer, with enough work to do and enough cash money, which he carried loose in his pockets, that he could afford to keep the boy scout, Bud Gentry, busy as his hired hand all summer.

But Joe Graff didn't look especially prosperous. He always wore bib overalls, a faded chambray shirt, a scuffed-up pair of workshoes, and stretched out cotton socks that had once been white. From one year to the next, he wore a sweat- stained, out-of-shape felt hat that was as likely to be used as a vessel for watering a thirsty horse as for shading his eyes. He told time by squinting at the sky and by reckoning what his belly told him about how long it was till mealtime.

There was a roll to Joe's gait and a squint to his eyes that bespoke of a lifetime of plowed ground and hot sun. His hairy-backed hands, his face, and his neck, down across the unbuttoned "V" of his shirt were burned a coppery brown that never faded in winter. The rest of his body, when it was uncovered for a rare soak in the number three galvanized tub, was as white and soft as a new baby's bottom.

But there wasn't anything soft about Joe Graff's character. He was known far and wide as a man you could depend on to do whatever needed doing. His word, the saying went, was worth the price of the finest farm in the county.

On the other hand, Andy Delhotal — they said it "da-LO-tel" — equally sunburned, but a good deal taller than Joe Graff, looked every inch a prosperous farmer.

He was most apt to be seen wearing a matched set of khaki-colored work pants and shirt that had started the day with starch, creases, and buttons all intact, a respectable pair of shoes which he paid his son, Lyle, to shine on Saturdays, and a decent straw hat, new every summer. He consulted a gold pocket watch when he wanted to know the time of day, paid for his beer from a pinch purse full of change, and carried a leather wallet for his folding money.

It was a Tuesday, and Andy Delhotal had been to the public sale at Chana, just south of Route 64, in Ogle County. A couple of good teams of horses had sold at Chana that day, and, afterward, the farmers had got to talking about their own teams. In the go-around, someone at the sale had made Andy a halfhearted offer to buy his team of matched Percherons. Andy had turned down the offer; the team wasn't for sale, but by the time he had driven home to Lee Center, he was feeling pretty puffed up about the offer.

As soon as he'd taken the head off his first bottle of beer, Andy commenced to bragging about his team, finally allowing that there wasn't a team in Lee County or any county Lee County touched that could out-pull his two-ton pair.

Joe Graff, of course, had been taking all of this in and suddenly he felt like he couldn't listen to any more. Turning slowly around to face Andy, he said, "Goddammit, Delhotal, ol' Buster, as wore out as he is, can out-pull any horse you got."

That quieted things down a bit as every eye in the place turned to look at Joe Graff, who turned back to the bar and took a long draw on his third beer.

"When you want this contest to take place?" asked Andy.

"Suit yerself," said Joe.

Before Russel Gentry's tavern closed that night, most of Lee Center had already heard that Joe Graff and Andy Delhotal would square off with a horse apiece at the Lee County Fair, which was then only a couple of weeks away.

Business was extra good that night as every man in Lee Center who could get out of his house stopped by the tavern to hear for himself that the contest was really on.

* * * * *

At the breakfast table the next morning, Joe Graff told his summer hand, Bud Gentry, that he could put off finishing the job of cleaning out the henhouse. Instead, he was to bring down Buster's harness and clean it up and sort out what Joe himself would have to mend. Then he was to polish up the metal parts of the harness as best he could.

"Buster's harness? I didn't know Buster had any harness, Mister Graff," the boy said.

"Well, he does," grunted Joe. "You'll have to get it down out of the loft, and you'll find a can of saddle soap in there where I keep the hoof trimmers and the linament. You can work that saddle soap into the leather real good, and ask Missus Graff for her box of Bon Ami to clean up the metal. I want them brass knobs shining like new silver dollars, and I'll get Skin Snell to make Buster a new pair of shoes."

"You ain't gitten Buster ready to sell, are you, Mister Graff?" Bud asked.

"No, I ain't," answered Joe. "I think the old boy's got about one more good pull left in him and I aim to give him a chance to prove it." And, with that, he told his Missus and Bud about the bargain he'd struck with Andy Delhotal the afternoon before.

So first thing after breakfast, Bud climbed up into the loft, found the harness, and tossed it down onto the barnfloor. Then he led Buster in, fitted the harness on him the best he could, and walked around the old horse, taking a good look.

84

The harness was in awfully sad shape, but it didn't seem to be much worse off than Buster.

Bud knew, probably better than anyone else did, just how bony the horse was, from the times he'd saddled him to ride to the pasture. Joe Graff had an out-of-date U.S. Army McClellan saddle he let Bud use; likely the only kind of saddle you could have put on Buster, for it had an open trench down the middle, where Buster's backbone came up through, almost level with the saddle's seat.

When Joe came to get the parts of the harness which needed mending, he saw Bud's face all screwed up with concern, but he didn't comment on it; he just took a big armful of the harness into his lean-to workroom, where he measured and cut and riveted for the better part of the day.

Bud started with Buster's collar and, as Joe Graff finished his mending and brought the parts into the barn, one at a time, the boy worked his way through the hames, the bellyband, and the breeches, the backstrap and the traces. He slathered on the saddle soap and felt the dried-out leather begin to come alive under the work of his hands. Since Buster would be pulling alone, Joe fashioned a martingale to reach from the front of the collar, down Buster's chest, and between his front legs to connect with the bellyband.

"His bridle is in terrible shape," Bud told Joe, but the farmer said not to worry about that; they wouldn't need a bridle.

Skin Snell, who did blacksmithing for the farmers, came by with a wooden apple box full of shoes to check Buster for size. It turned out he didn't have to make new shoes, though; he just took Buster's castoff irons back to his forge to straighten them out. The next day he came back and trimmed and filed Buster's front hooves and nailed the shoes on.

Bud thought maybe the horse carried his head just a tad

higher after Skin finished shoeing him.

Over the next week, Bud worried a lot about the contest. He knew Buster hadn't been in harness during any time he could remember, and he was just flat out scared the tired, bony horse couldn't compete with whatever Andy Dehlotal showed up with. Everybody knew Andy kept a fine stable of horses, two teams and a couple of spares, and nobody doubted for a minute that he'd trot out the best of the lot when the time came.

Joe Graff sensed what was on Bud's mind. Finally, he told him, "Buddy, there ain't nothing more we can do. Either Buster's got it or he hain't, and all we can do now is be there and give him a chance."

* * * * *

There wasn't much draw to the county fair for Bud that year. The midway, the rides, even the livestock exhibits just didn't hold much excitement, compared to what everyone seemed to be talking about and waiting for, the contest between Buster and Andy Delhotal's best horse, a one-ton sorrel gelding.

The horse pulling contests were to be held on the third day of the fair, and the special challenge pull was set for the last feature of the day, the fair officials realizing a lot of people would hang around the fairgrounds to watch it. That was good, for it gave Bud time to be there, after school, which had already begun its fall session.

Bud's grandpa, John Gentry, and his grandma, Grace, picked him up at the schoolhouse and they hurried to the fairgrounds, where they climbed into good seats in the grandstand. All around them, little knots of men stood around, talking about the contest and making bets on the

86

outcome, and Bud was glad to hear that some of them were putting money on Buster.

As the horse which had been challenged, Andy's gelding would lead off the competition. Andy, with fresh creases in his pants and a cocky set to his second new straw hat that summer, appeared, leading the favorite. Andy's shiny, freshly blackened shoes heeled into the churned up dirt and his shoulders leaned back as he hauled on the reins. It looked like he had about all he could do to keep his eager horse in check.

The gelding's hide caught the sun and glowed. His black leather harness gleamed like brand new, and the brass studding and hame knobs glinted as if they were made of solid gold. Snappy red ribbons gathered his mane into dainty tassles which stood up along his neckspine. Another red ribbon was laced through the dark tail, its bow and streamers fluttering as the gelding, a real crowd pleaser, switched his tail with every proud step he made.

Andy unbuckled the check reins from the brass eyelets in the collarpiece and hooked them to hang loose on the bridle. The horse tossed his head and snorted as Andy pulled on the reins and backed him up to the heavy, wooden sled, where he fastened the traces to the singletree.

Alongside the horse and reaching out in front of him, an inch-thick cable stretched toward a heavy post, set into the sod, over a hundred feet away. The other end of the cable was fastened to another post set into the ground behind the sled, which was in back of the horse and off to the side. At intervals along the cable were fifty-pound concrete blocks with the cable threaded through them. The horse would be guided along the cable, picking up the concrete weights onto the sled as he came to them.

It was pretty well the standard in pulling contests

involving big horses that they'd pull their own weight with their weight; that is, they'd pull that much before they'd have to knuckle down and throw their muscle into the job. The sled already held 900 pounds of the concrete blocks, just a hundred pounds short of half the gelding's weight.

The horse had been here before and was anxious to get started, stomping some, throwing his head, and snorting now and then. Andy looked around to make sure everyone was clear of the sled and the cable, gave a little snap to the reins, and said, "GITup."

Everybody strained forward in their seats to watch as the horse started to move. John Gentry leaned over his grandson's ear and whispered, "Now, watch close, Buddy. He'll walk off with the first eighteen blocks, and then he'll begin to feel it. He'll stop at twenty-two, because that horse won't pull more than his own weight."

Although he didn't say how he knew what he thought the horse would pull, it was well known there probably wasn't a better judge of horseflesh in the stands that day than John Gentry. Coming from a natural line of auctioneers, he had presided over farm and public auction sales for most of his adult life. He could pretty well take the measure of a horse with a single walk around, a look at its teeth, and a couple of whacks on the beast's hip and shoulder. What he said now made Bud feel a little bit better about the possible limitations of the Delhotal horse, but he still had reservations about what Buster could do.

Sure enough, the big sorrel walked down the cable like he was leading a parade, and the blocks stacked up on the sled behind him. The first dozen were nothing; they just slid into place. Numbers 13 and 14 made a definite clunk as they settled; 15 and 16 made double clunks, first as the sled hit them, and then again, as they slammed into place, but the horse didn't really slow down. As the sled hit the seventeenth block, a whuff escaped the horse's nostrils and the whuff was a little louder with the eighteenth. There was just a hint of a pause at Number 19, and a little more of a pause at 20, but both blocks slid back next to the others on the wooden sled.

As they approached Number 21, the horse slowed down some. Andy hollered "GitUP!" and the big sorrel slapped the sled into the block, and picked it up. He looked like he might miss a step as he leaned into the harness on the way to Number 22, so Andy put his lungs into it. He hollered, "GIT HUP THERE!" and his horse stretched out, covered the space, slammed into the weight, and kept going as the concrete block crunched back onto the sled. Then he took a couple of steps forward, and stopped, like Andy had pulled on the reins, only everybody knew he hadn't.

"Ya see there, Buddy?" whispered his grandpa.

When the big sorrel gelding stopped, he began to sweat, and his brown coat took on a wet shine. "All right, boy; you GEEE-IT HUP!" hollered Andy, and the horse strained into the harness, but didn't move. His full weight lay on the sled behind him, and nothing Andy could say, over the yelling of the crowd, could make the horse pull another foot.

Everybody who had their money on Andy's horse felt pretty good about it, for in a call-out pull of this kind, the challenger, in order to win, had to go one farther than the weight the first horse had pulled. Right now, that meant that Buster would have to walk off with at least 23 blocks over and above the beginning 900 pounds, and that would be a good deal over Buster's weight. Right that minute, if the truth were known, there probably wasn't a person on the fairgrounds who wasn't doubting it would happen.

With the possible exception, maybe, of Joe Graff.

Joe had worked Buster in the horse's prime. He knew that

in spite of the way Buster looked, there was still some gristle in him; he was a big-boned animal to begin with, and he'd never really been off his feed; he'd just kind of relaxed on good pasture. And, deep down, Joe Graff knew that when it came to having a heart for doing a job, he and Buster had been pretty well matched. He also knew that, win or lose, this day wasn't going to make a terrible lot of difference in the life of either him or his horse, so they might just as well give it a good go.

Satisfied with what his horse had done, Andy Delhotal unbuckled the traces and, with everybody cheering, he guided the gelding off to the side, and motioned for his boys to come out and start rubbing the horse down.

The contest crew hitched a team onto the rear of the sled to pull it back to the starting place. While one man walked and held the reins, the other rode the sled, kicking off the cement blocks at their stations as the sled moved along.

Then, from behind the trailer he'd brought his horse to the fairgrounds in, came Joe Graff, leading Buster, and everyone in the crowd took in their breath. The loudest gasp Bud Gentry heard came from his grandma, sitting beside him, straight as a ramrod and wearing her little navy blue hat with the pheasant feather slanted over one eye.

"That poor old horse," Grandma Gentry was heard to say. "That crazy man'll kill him, right here in front of us."

Without looking away from Joe and Buster, John said, "Now, Mother, the man knows what he's doing."

Bud pulled on John's sleeve. "Grandpa, Mister Graff ain't even got a bit in Buster's mouth. Ain't he gonna put no bridle on him?"

"Must think he doesn't need one. That hackamore is gentle on him, gives him less to worry about, but reminds him he's in harness. It's probably what he was trained with, when

90

he was a colt. Joe knows what he's doing."

Joe was wearing his overalls and his scuffed up shoes and his sweat stained, dilapidated hat, like he'd just come from the barn. Behind him, with a lead rope fastened to a light hackamore halter, plodded Buster.

There was no check rein, and his head swung from side to side with each step. His mouth was working like it was full of something he couldn't swallow, and each of his big feet rose and clopped into the dust as though it was independent of the other three. The new brass rivets glinted in all the places where Joe had mended the harness, and nobody probably would have even noticed the hame knobs Bud had worked at with the Bon Ami, except for the fact that the reins were looped up over them.

Buster stopped in front of the sled, for he had been here too, a long time ago.

Joe tossed his lead rope up over the knobs with the reins and said, quietly, "Back up, Buster." Buster stepped into place and Joe walked back and hitched him to the singletree. Looking around to make sure everyone was clear of the sled and the cable, Joe placed a light slap on the horse's hip, stepped off to the side, and said, kinda quiet, "Okay, Buster. Git."

Buster's head came up, the slack went out of his harness, and he began to move down the cable, picking up the concrete blocks. It seemed like he just set his eyes on the post at the other end and had nothing on his mind but walking toward it. There was quiet in the grandstand.

Ten of the blocks slid into place behind Buster before he began to look like it might be work, but he kept on walking, and he kept on picking up weights.

By the time he picked up the sixteenth block, he had begun to hunker down and put a strain on his legs. There

91

were seventeen hundred pounds on the sled. Here and there, farmers ciphered on their palms with inkless index fingers and figured Buster must be pretty close to pulling his own weight. When Buster picked up the next block, easing into his collar and straining with his shoulders and thighs, his front feet were grabbing dirt.

With 17 behind him and working hard, Buster approached Number 18 and it chunked onto the sled. The horse's eyes had taken on a frightened look. His tongue was hanging out and working like it might be able to help some. Muscles nobody thought the ancient horse had, hardened and stretched; Buster hunkered down a little more, and kept moving forward.

Number 19 slid onto the wood frame of the sled and inched into place. Buster's belly was quivering only a foot from the ground when he edged up on Number 20 and scooped it onto the sled.

It looked like Buster was just about giving it everything he had as he came up on 21, with only it and one more block to go to make him equal with the big sorrel. The sled lurched when it made contact with the block.

As soon as it slammed into place, Joe Graff said, real quiet, "Whoa, Buster." The old horse relaxed some, but he didn't stand all the way up.

"Is he quitting, Grandpa?" Bud wanted to know.

"No; just watch," his granddad replied.

On Bud's other side, his grandma, stoic that she always seemed to be, was getting some worked up. "He'll kill that horse. Right here in front of us, he'll kill him," she said, in a loud whisper.

This time, when John Gentry said, "Now, Mother," he reached across his grandson, without ever looking away from the horse, and briefly touched his wife's hand. Bud couldn't remember ever having seen his grandpa do such a thing.

Joe patted Buster on the flank and walked off to one side, where there was a bucket of water. He hauled off his hat, scooped it full of water, and went back to Buster. The horse was blowing air something powerful, and his withers were whuffing like a bellows. He was beginning to make a strange noise similar to his whinny.

When Joe held the hatful of water up in front of him, Buster didn't really drink. He just kind of played in the water a little, splashing and cooling off his mouth. When he quit, Joe poured the rest of the water over Buster's head and put his hat back in place. He stroked the horse once or twice on the side and flank as he walked past him, and then stepped off to the side.

A brief mumbling, like a stick moving in a wooden bucketful of ripe grain, was heard to stir among the watchers, but nothing was said for ears farther than the next pair away.

Joe Graff turned to face Buster and, in a tone of voice like he was talking to an old friend, he said, "All right, now, Buster. You GIT!"

With a mighty strain, Buster went down on his hunkers and began to move. He picked up Block Number 22, which made him even with his competition, but nobody cheered, as you might expect them to, for Buster still had work to do. He staggered under the weight and it appeared, for a moment, like he might slow down.

All of a sudden, Joe Graff whistled.

Nobody had any idea Joe Graff could whistle; he didn't have any teeth to whistle through, but he made the most piercing sound you ever heard in your life, and Buster answered it with everything he had.

The horse went down, scrambling, his belly clean to the ground. He was pulling with every muscle he had in his hindquarters and, up front, he was pushing his straining chest into his collar. Forgotten muscles that hadn't been used in years, from his neck through his withers and shoulders, down his front legs to where his remade shoes were digging out eight-inch furrows in the dirt; across his back and loins, down his hips to his hacks, and then bending on down to his hind feet. Those big unshod hind feet would jump forward and dig in, jump forward and dig in, making a few inches with each jump. His harness was slapping against his wet hide, and a mighty snort was whuffing out of his nostrils in each split second between the jumps.

He kept that up, inch by inch, coming up on that twenty-third block. The dust was so thick it covered the block and the cable and flew in Buster's face, and nobody in the grandstand could tell just how close they were till they heard the chunk and the scratching sound as the weight slid onto the sled and made its way back to lie against the rest.

It took a second or two for everybody to react and while it was still quiet, Joe Graff's "Whoa, Buster" made the old horse relax.

Joe went to his head, took the lead rein down from the hameknob, and urged Buster to his feet. As he stood there, whacking the horse on the neck, the crowd went wild, whistling, and hollering, and clapping their hands. Right next to him, Bud Gentry heard his grandma say, "Look at them, Buddy. Just look at them. Darned old fools."

Bud looked where his grandma was looking, toward the men who were starting to angle down out of the bleachers. Some of them were already walking toward Buster, and almost every one of them had tears sparkling in the crinkles of his eyes or just plain running down his face.

Later, it was said there wasn't a man there with money on Andy Delhotal's horse that minded giving it up, after what

94

he'd just seen.

*　　*　　*　　*　　*

Buster was trucked home that day and turned back out to pasture and, if such was possible, it seemed the old horse perked up some, like maybe he had something new to chew over. He took to hanging around the barn more, where people came to make a fuss over him and just to look him over.

There had been a reporter with a camera at the contest, and the picture he took of Buster, bellied down and straining, at the moment he bested Andy Delhotal's sorrel gelding, appeared in the next day's edition of the *Dixon Telegraph*. Framed, it hung on the wall of the office at the grain elevator in Lee Center for many years.

The legend of Old Buster stayed alive in Lee County, Illinois, for a long time, and the boys of Bud Gentry's generation took the story across the United States and around the world. Bud himself described the contest to a sailor on deckwatch on a Great Lakes oreboat, and he watched its telling bring tears to the eyes of a penful of toughened bull riders at a rodeo in Yankee Stadium. He talked about Buster on dark nights when the enemy stayed at bay in Korea and Vietnam.

He told it to me for the first time on our honeymoon, in 1968, as we traveled across America's heartland, getting acquainted with one another's past.

It will always be the best animal story I ever heard.

GYPSY

Muffin had been a member of his family for almost as long as David Burns could remember. The gentle, even-tempered, mostly collie puppy had been little more than a baby when she had come from the animal shelter, straight into the hearts of David and his parents, Dr. Eddy and Penny Burns.

Muffin was a lady whose behavior never had any serious lapses. She was his constant companion while David was growing up, and somehow he never questioned whether it would always be so.

Then, some time after the Christmas holidays during his sophomore year at Georgia State, David learned that Muffin, almost seventeen years old, had died. He hated to think what home would be like without her and, sure enough, when he arrived on spring break, his family's lovely home in old northeast Saint Petersburg just wasn't the same.

So, on the second day of vacation, David drove out into the country and, at the SPCA shelter, just off Starkey Road, he made a choice which was to change his family's lives and perhaps the course of some very historic events.

Walking through the long rows of well tended pens that day, David wanted almost every dog he saw, for each of them appealed to him in some special way. Until he saw the little black Lab.

Straining awkwardly to reach through the bars of the cage, her big ears folded forward, the puppy's snappy dark eyes seemed to be taking in everything around her — and all at once.

David thought she looked like she was expecting something to happen; perhaps, even, as though she had been wound up and was waiting to be turned on.

David spoke to her. The turn-on occurred and, for the next year and a half, nobody thought she would ever run down.

Nothing in Muffin's quiet and gentle ways had prepared any of the family for the pure physical onslaught of the puppy. She was never still; she never wanted to settle down in one place and, before her first day with them had ended, the Burnses agreed that the only name which suited the snappy-eyed, little on-the-go dog was Gypsy.

She was just past babyhood and small, except for her big feet — almost scrawny, as though she had been underfed, but she lacked nothing in stamina or aggressiveness. The very first time she was told, "No-no," she responded with sassy backtalk, and she never let up. Everything about her marked her as a tough little girl.

Spring break soon ended and with David's return to college in Atlanta, care and responsibility for the feisty little dog was transferred to his mother.

Penny Burns enrolled Gypsy in obedience classes and when the two of them went off to the first day of school, the mistress was full of hope. The dog — well, the dog was a mobile exhibit of raw energy. Penny held fast to the looped end of a brand new red leather leash; Gypsy tugged unceasingly at the other end. Proud that her son had selected a dog with the well-documented possibilities of a Labrador retriever, Penny fully expected Gypsy to finish the course as a well-behaved, well-adjusted dog, probably at the head of her class.

But, after the first fifteen minutes of the first class, it was obvious that Gypsy had her heart set upon failing the course. She would not be trained. She would not sit; she would not stay; she simply would not perform on command. Instead, she wanted to dominate every other dog in the class, regardless of its age or size.

She ate the course textbook.

Back home, perhaps to show that she would not be controlled by it, Gypsy ate the red leather leash.

She ate her Scot's plaid L. L. Bean bed. And a pair of her mistress's favorite shoes, red leather heels Penny had splurged to own. She ate a piece of the couch in the den. The foxholes she dug in the back yard, Penny was sure, would have hidden a battalion of United States Marines.

"She's just so dominant, so hyper, so . . . bad," Penny told a friend.

Gypsy didn't hide any of her bad deeds or show any remorse at their discovery, as one might expect a bad actor to do. She brazenly left the shreds of the red leather shoes on the bedroom carpet; she looked up only momentarily when Penny walked into the den, then returned to the job of tearing up the sofa. The metal parts of the leather leash which she could not destroy, she discarded on the tiles of the kitchen floor.

Even Penny herself was not safe, as Gypsy repaid her petting by gnawing Penny's hands, wrists, and ankles.

Before long, veterinary bills were added to the costs of maintaining the puppy when Gypsy, after making her way onto a shelf in the garage, was found playing with a box of poison which had been bought to combat citrus rats. The box had been chewed open and it simply could not be determined whether some of the contents were missing, so Gypsy was taken to have her stomach pumped and to spend the night at the animal hospital.

In desperation, Penny Burns engaged the professional services of a dog behaviorist to privately tutor the rambunctious Gypsy and to counsel her owners. By the end of Diane Dunne's second visit, she concluded that the Burnses had acquired, in Gypsy, what experts have termed an Alpha dog; that is, one which is inherently endowed with a dominating personality.

As if Eddy and Penny Burns hadn't already guessed.

If she had been a member of a wild or feral pack, the counselor said, Gypsy would have been instantly recognized as the group's dominant female. As a house pet, she dominated her human family, as well as any and all other subjects with which she came into contact.

It was simply Gypsy's way.

They could find no way of training "out" or "around" the all-pervading trait.

When she left, after her third visit, Diane Dunne left behind pamphlets which discussed the Alpha Dog Syndrome, hoping Eddy and Penny might find something in them which would help them deal with their problem dog.

Gypsy ate the pamphlets, and the Burnses at last acknowledged they had adopted what they now came to accept as an unredeemably naughty dog.

What to do with or about Gypsy became the haunting problem of their lives, and there seemed to be no good solution.

Finding a new owner for Gypsy was, of course, at the top of the list of possibilities, but Eddy and Penny could think of no one to whom they could entrust the rapidly maturing dog who might not, ultimately, mistreat her for her failure to accept discipline.

The possibility of having her put to sleep occurred to them but, this, too, was out of the question, for Penny had come to love the innately playful, obviously intelligent little dog in spite of her rascality. Failure to behave simply was not sufficient reason to impose a death sentence upon her.

In the face of an ever growing mountain of evidence, Penny found herself, time and again, having to defend her support of Gypsy. At last, even her patient husband seemed inclined to wash his hands of interest or responsibility for the dog.

Gypsy's treatment of Eddy himself did nothing to dispel his growing frustration with her or to make the dog's position in the household, as far as he was concerned, any more secure. When she heard his car come into the garage, at the end of the day, Gypsy would position herself in some unexpected place, wait for him to enter the room, and then, dashing with the speed of a runaway train, she would crash into him, throwing him off balance with the surprise and the sheer weight of the encounter.

When Eddy sounded what seemed to be a thinly-veiled warning about the possibility of his wife's developing a neurosis over the little dog, Penny consented to a trial separation.

The Burnses made reservations amd packed for a two weeks' trip to England. When the date of departure arrived, they booked Gypsy into a boarding kennel suggested by their veterinarian. With only slightly less guilt than she'd have felt at deserting the dog entirely, Penny mused that a couple of weeks in jail might just help Gypsy to appreciate her good home. On the other hand, she knew that when the brief respite came to an end, some solution to Gypsy's future would have

100

to be found.

In mid-flight, somewhere over the Atlantic, Nancy Siver, who was traveling with the Burnses, suddenly came alive from an article she was reading in a copy of the *American Kennel Club Gazette*. Nancy, a Saint Petersburg breeder of English Springer Spaniels, who had been familiar with Gypsy's story since its beginning, had come upon an article which asked the pointed question, "Do you have a bad Lab?"

Quickly scanning the article, and then reading it again, more slowly, Penny Burns decided that the author was talking about Gypsy. Debby Kay, then of Herndon, Virginia, and president of International Detective Dogs, Limited, trained dogs for drug and explosive detection. She had written the Gazette article hoping to expand the recruitment of applicants for her school, and she seemed to describe exactly the Alpha Dog personality of Gypsy as her quarry.

The possibility this opened for the Burnses lent an unexpected excitement to their trip, and they vowed to contact Debby Kay immediately upon their return.

*   *   *   *   *

Two weeks later, back in the states, a single phone call confirmed that Gypsy was, indeed, the kind of animal Debby Kay had in mind, and an appointment was made for a personal interview in Gypsy's home.

Gypsy responded to the woman as she had to no other person and, within minutes of her arrival, Debby Kay and Gypsy were playing fetch, with an old towel, in the backyard.

"She just loved Gypsy," Penny said, "and wanted to know if we could locate the rest of the litter." That, of course, was impossible.

Debby spent the better part of an hour sharing with the Burnses a scrapbook which highlighted her successes with dogs such as Gypsy. At the end of the interview, Penny and Eddie were so completely satisfied with Debby's ability in handling this kind of dog that they agreed to turn the little black Labrador over to her.

With a total of fifty canine "interviews" to be conducted before returning to Virginia, Debby left Gypsy with the Burns household in order that a current physical exam could be done and her rabies shots brought up to date. A day in November was set for her return to take Gypsy to Virginia for trial testing.

On the morning Debby Kay was to return, Penny backed the family's Mercedes out of the garage and she and Gypsy went for their last ride together, to the veterinarian's office.

On the return journey, with the newly signed paperwork certifying Gypsy's good health and the currency of her vaccinations, Penny had the first hint of misgiving about what they were doing. During the ride, at the veterinarian's office, and now, headed home again, Gypsy was being good. She sat quietly in the passenger seat, looking out the window, with an occasional friendly glance in Penny's direction. It was just enough to make Penny Burns wonder if they had, indeed, tried everything possible which might help Gypsy fit into their lives.

Penny needed to make one brief stop, and did so, leaving the young dog in the car. When she returned to the car, Gypsy was sitting serenely in the right-hand seat, waiting quietly for Penny's return. As Penny started the car's engine, the doubt returned. Perhaps — just perhaps — they had acted too quickly, she thought, as she settled behind the wheel.

Then she reached to shift the engine into gear and encountered naked metal, coated with saliva. During her brief

102

absence, Gypsy had eaten the beige leather cover of the gearshift knob. The growing doubt was gone, replaced by frustrated tears.

Even so, there were tears of another kind when it was time, later that day, to say goodbye and to watch as Debby Kay drove her van out of the Burnes' driveway, taking the indomitable Gypsy with her.

*   *   *   *   *

Soon, there began a series of long-distance calls to check on Gypsy's progress. Penny learned that, out of the fifty scheduled interviews, Gypsy had been one of only seven dogs which had qualified to begin basic training at the Virginia school for detector dogs.

During the first weeks at the training kennel, when the new dogs were observed as they enjoyed the freedom of International's protected runs, Gypsy immediately became the dominant member of her class. She became especially attached to a reclusive "homesick" dog which seemed determined to separate itself from the other canine applicants. Gypsy delighted Debby by urging the lonesome dog into a closer association with the group, thus saving it from rejection from the course, an option which was being considered.

When actual training began, Gypsy was soon singled out as the star pupil. She was swifter than her larger breed relations, consistently out running and out jumping the heavier, truer-to-breed Labs.

On the telephone, Debby Kay waxed technical. "Gypsy's a wonderful dog. She's super agile; she has just the right bone-to-muscle ratio for the work, and her size makes her free of the threat of hip dysplasia, a hip abnormality which can

103

become crippling and is peculiar to larger dogs." She indicated this was especially important in the training regimen of her dogs, for a lot of jumping into trucks and over fences would be required of them.

She explained she had determined Gypsy was part whippet, "and they don't get dysplasia." She said this had reinforced an idea she was entertaining of cross breeding Labradors, shepherds, and golden retrievers with whippets for detector dogs. Large dogs, she added, are best for work of this kind because they have a more highly developed sense of smell.

Early in its instruction, a decision must be made for each dog, whether it shall be trained to report the finding of drugs or explosives. It would simply be impractical for an animal to be trained for both, since most often it is necessary to evacuate an entire building when explosives are found, whereas a confined search area can be maintained when a dog gives notice of the presence of hidden narcotics.

Gypsy, it was determined, would be trained to detect the presence of explosives.

The course was finally completed. Debby Kay was satisfied with the dog's ability, and Gypsy was graduated as a fully-qualified explosive detector canine.

"Now what?" Penny Burns wondered. How would Gypsy's newly proven abilities be used?

One of the last steps of Gypsy's training, that springtime of 1988, was learning to accept commands in a new language — Korean. And that summer Gypsy was flown halfway around the world to that far eastern country.

There, the little black dog which had been described as hyper, dominant, untrainable, and just plain naughty, fulfilled the very important job of helping to make sure the Summer Olympic Games were safe from the threat of hidden bombs.

The Burnses, and everyone else who had known Gypsy, nearly popped their buttons with pride in the willful dog that had finally realized her potential.

FALLEN ANGEL

Christmas was more than a week away when, at dinner with our friends, Frank and Jackie Williams and their sons, our Godchild Andrew and his brother Chris, Bud and I were drawn into a discussion about arrangements for Tiger's Christmas.

Andrew's cocker spaniel, Snuffy, would accompany the members of the family for a month's skiing at Steamboat Springs, in Colorado, but there seemed no way to accommodate Tiger, the ten-week-old gray-striped kitten who shared a newly acquired apartment with Chris across town.

The problem was unresolved when we left the Williamses that night, and the next morning, at breakfast, I wondered aloud how Barney and Thai would take to having a kitten underfoot for a couple of weeks. When I called Jackie and suggested our keeping Tiger, she was thrilled. Chris, in turn, was ecstatic, and the problem was solved. We would keep the kitten which, at ten weeks, would be hardly more than a baby.

Now, it was the Friday before Christmas. I had just put the finishing touches on the Christmas tree when Chris came by to drop off the little cat.

I took the kitten from his owner's arms and, hugging the tabby's silken coat to my cheek, I prophesied, "There's nothing like a kitten under a Christmas tree."

The kitten's eyes traveled swiftly past the tiny lighted

church and the schoolhouse, paused only briefly upon the wee silk rocking horse, the whimsical elves, and the painted porcelain bells, all dangling among the fragrant green needles. Eyes dancing with the reflected gleam from hundreds of tiny colored lamps, his gaze seemed to go directly to the top of the tree where a very special angel was set to preside over her twenty-seventh Christmas.

The royal red velvet of her gem-spattered gown, the soft waxen smile, her tiny gold crown, and the golden tree she offered in outstretched arms — even the tasseled, golden tag proclaiming her pedigree as a Koestel, first family of treetop angels — all proclaimed the perfection with which she had long ago been imbued.

So lovely was this hostess of so many Christmases that holiday guests failed to notice the tiny pinpoints of light glinting where a kitten's needley teeth first tested the feather-patterned foil of one of her wings.

The kitten had been Charlie, an adopted stray, and the year had been 1965.

As a loving mother guards against the revelation of her child's faults, I had shown no one the tiny pins which pierced the angel's shoulder, holding in place that same perforated wing, torn off by another kitten in a lightning moment while my back was turned.

Hannibal, 1969.

Yearly, I had replaced the cellophane tape, mending a jagged tear in that singular golden pinion.

Barney, 1973.

Of all the kittens who had seen the parade of Christmases, only Thai had left the Koestel angel's wing unmarked. Herself so scarred from babyhood by the terror of abuse that she never learned to play, she yearly watched the winking, lighted tree, not deigning to disturb so much as a single ornament.

When I put him down, Tiger explored the limits of his temporary home, sampled the contents of the water bowl in the kitchen, and sniffed where a food dish had lately been. Then he was brought to the place where Barney and Thai were gathered for the Receiving Of The Bows.

After many years' habit (seventeen, at that time, for Barney; fourteen for Thai), they posed impressively to receive, each, a badge of the season. Cut new each year from whatever mostly-red fabric my sewing box may yield, the inch-wide ribbons of cloth fray slightly with the wearing, making sure they remain tied and in place throughout the days of the Christmas season.

Tiger watched as the bows were adjusted upon the aristocratic necks of his two new Siamese friends and squirmed only feebly to receive his own.

For the next two days, red ribbon intact, he clambered over the brightly tied Christmas packages, cavorted upon the furniture, forbidden to his elders, and watched in wonder when a squirrel accepted peanuts from my hand at the back door. He left these milder pursuits to leap and tumble and reach and climb in all the places denied the older cats by a simple, "No," and to terrorize Barney and Thai with his constant playfulness.

Frequently he was scolded for batting ornaments from the lowest branches of the tree and, once, I disentangled him from a string of silver beads he'd grasped and carried, galloping, toward the next room, leaving the tree with a critical slant. Minor considerations, at Christmastime, when there's a kitten in the house.

On Christmas morning, I was called from the kitchen by a terrible clatter, and hurried to the livingroom to see every plaything on the tree swinging and turning, and jiggling again into place.

The Koestel angel was gone, and Tiger was nowhere to be seen. I searched for him quietly, rather than give vent to sudden anger on Christmas morning.

When I bent to peer into the darkness under the sofa, the two pinpoints of light which peered back at me were Tiger's eyes. The shiny thing protruding from his mouth was the tip of the angel's wing. She lay elsewhere, secure and unharmed, except for the shattered wing which kittens have attacked repeatedly during her lifetime.

When our guests arrived for Christmas dinner, the Koestel angel reigned serenely from the top of the tree, never mind a slightly shortened, much battered left wing.

Tiger, 1990.

AL NICE

The thirty years which had spanned my friendship with Charlotte Iles, a friendship enjoyed, sometimes across town and, sometimes across the miles of several states, had been marked by her often-changing company of stray cats and dogs. I wasn't particularly surprised, therefore, when she called from her home in South Carolina, to tell me she'd adopted a greyhound — a retired racing greyhound.

She said the adoption agency hadn't told her much about the dog, except that he'd had a successful career on the track, that he enjoyed good health, and exhibited a friendly disposition. The agency had told her that, without the offer of a home in which to spend his retirement, the dog would be put to death. After that, she hadn't bothered to ask how old the dog was or where he had raced and, of course, she was right that the answers to those questions weren't really important.

I asked her where she kept him, and she said, "In the house." Charlotte chuckled. "There wasn't any point," she continued, "in building a pen of any fence the city of Aiken would license, for a dog which could jump six feet straight up from a standing start." So the dog simply shared the house and yard with her and Boss, the yellow Lab, and the two one-time stray cats, Tiger and Bells.

The greyhound's well-chosen name, which had come with

him from his racing past, was Al Nice. It matched his gentlemanly behavior, his neat, quiet habits, and his ability to quickly transfer to Charlotte his apparently inborn sense of loyalty to the supplier of his needs.

He walked regally at leash, she said, and freed from restraint, he fetched whatever object she chose to toss. He had quickly accepted as his own the large blanket she provided and made his bed upon it, wherever Charlotte placed it in keeping with her own convenience. He minded his manners at the food bowl and was always polite and friendly with the other animals.

The only time Al Nice had exhibited behavior she could not control, Charlotte told me, was on the occasion of their first visit to her veterinarian. The moment she had opened the door to the vet's waiting room, the dog had nearly yanked the loop of his leash from her hand as he had tugged to set himself free.

Wondering what had brought on this sudden strange behavior, Charlotte had made certain there were no other animals in sight that Al Nice might be wanting to mix it up with, and dropped the leather strap. Freed, the dog had walked calmly across the room and stepped upon the vet's scale to be weighed, just as he had done every day of his former well-ordered life. It was then she discovered that, from his lean racing weight of 51 pounds, he had risen, with his new, easier lifestyle, to a comfortable 72.

Al Nice was a joy to have around, my friend said; there was but a single defect in his personality. Obviously, she said, greyhounds had been so finely bred for their racing ability that other traits had apparently simply been bred out.

"Like what?" I asked.

"Like ordinary smarts," my friend explained. "He doesn't think like other dogs. I can put him in a room and I don't even have to tell him to stay. I can just put any old box or a chair in the middle of the door and he hasn't got sense enough to figure out that he could just go around it or jump over it, or whatever. He'll stay in that room until I move the chair. He can't think for himself. I've never had a dog like that."

I thought that sounded strange, but I'd never met a greyhound so I couldn't think what I might say in the dog's defense. Smart or not, though, I'd heard enough to make me certain that Al Nice was a dog I wanted to meet.

* * * * * * *

So it was, that one morning a few months later, I said goodbye to home, husband, and cats, drove quietly over the long Howard Franklin Bridge spanning Tampa Bay and, midway through the sleeping city of Tampa, turned northward toward the Georgia state line.

Leaving the interstate at Tifton, I drove leisurely through the Georgia countryside, stopping just beyond Hunger and Hardship Creek, northeast of Dublin, to look at an ancient round barn. Its red paint was all but gone; summer climbers were spreading green over its tin conical roof; even the boards, long-since nailed over its broken windows, showed the wear of many seasons.

It had been a hundred and fifty years since the round country barn had come into use in America. Its popularity, alas, had not endured as well as this example of its art had, for the shape had proved wasteful and impractical; neither animals nor food nor machinery could be conveniently stored in its pie-shaped rooms. As much a part of Americana as dog-racing, though, I thought, and I drove on, my thoughts returning to the subject of my journey.

At the world-famous Derby Lanes, in Saint Petersburg, and at tracks in Tampa and Sarasota, I had watched the lean and nervous greyhounds break from their starting gates to chase an artificial white cotton rabbit, bouncing ahead of them on a clicking metal contraption. I had wondered how, day after day, they could be fooled into believing that they chased a real rabbit.

After learning about Al Nice and hearing from Charlotte some of the surprises a racing dog brings to its retirement, I had sought out a greyhound kennel owner near the Saint Petersburg track, and asked if I could come out and talk with her. I was really curious about what makes these fascinating dogs tick.

I had heard that a racing greyhound is persuaded to habits of obedience through fear of repeated harsh treatment. I had heard, also, that racing greyhounds are deliberately starved to keep them lean and hungry; that the prospect of making a meal of the white cotton rabbit is the incentive for its swift chase, and I couldn't help wondering how that fact, if true, might fit in with Charlotte's contention that common dog sense has been "bred out" of greyhounds. Surely, it seemed, the dogs must know they are chasing a thing which is not alive.

I was not at all sure I'd actually be allowed to see these feisty, temperamental dogs close up; I doubted I'd be let in on such secrets as the withholding of food and the masking of dogs before a race to protect handlers from their nasty tempers — tempers made worse by taunting and meanness on the part of those same handlers — a device to arouse the dog's anger and competitive spirit.

All of these harsh-sounding means of controlling the working greyhound had been represented as truths.

Daylight had not yet broken when Audrey Alderson

113

welcomed me into her kennel, located hard by Derby Lane, at Saint Petersburg, Florida. She and her staff were just beginning their day, and as I followed her around for the better part of the morning, getting to know her and her dogs, and the ways in which they were cared for, I developed a deep respect for this lady and her work.

The thirty adult racing dogs and a like number of puppies I met there are maintained in the finest sort of clean, fresh-smelling kennels. Their needs are seen to by a crew of grooms and handlers who know what they're doing and care deeply about the well being and the healthy frame of mind of their charges. Only quality ingredients went into the food I watched Audrey prepare for her dogs. It contained carefully measured and blended amounts of meat, bulk, vitamins, and minerals.

I studied the charts where each animal was painstakingly kept account of, with races scheduled at intervals which would allow its very best care and fitness. With the exactness of the attention given to first-class human athletes, the dogs scheduled to go on the track that day were offered a specialized meal which would prepare them for their energy-depleting run. And each dog would know, from habit, that another special meal would be waiting when it returned from the day's race, with extra goodies for a winner!

Every dog in the kennel could be plainly seen to have a heads-up feeling about its own importance and value. Each dog responded quickly to the sound of its name. And every time one of the dogs made contact with a human, there was a friendly exchange. The owner or worker patted or stroked the animal. The dog, in turn, made quick licks on hands, arms, and, when possible, the face of any close-enough human.

Immediately, I was included in this happy give-and-take and, from the actions of these well cared for animals, I was

114

not surprised when the owner told me that every dog and every puppy in her kennel received at least one good hug every day.

These were no signs of poor treatment, overwork, fear, or starvation.

I watched as dogs due for training runs that morning hurried their trainers to the sandlot, eager to pull out all the stops and release their incredible stores of energy in fantastic dashes over the carefully controlled course.

I learned that a racer is muzzled for an appearance on the track to protect other dogs, in case one decides to take its competitiveness too seriously and fend off a rival.

I had gone home, after my visit to the kennel, pleased and content with everything I had seen, and now, remembering the experience, I was eager for my meeting with Al Nice.

My reverie had carried me across the summering landscape of Georgia and, before long, I crossed the historic Savannah River and climbed the hill into Aiken. Skirting the pine-woods campus of the University of South Carolina, I arrived at my friend's home.

When I got out of the car, a large, yellow dog raised his bulk from the doorstep and came to nuzzle my hand. This was Boss, the loving and loveable Lab, a former stray. From inside the house, I heard the familiar voice of my friend, as she shouted, "You're here!"

Charlotte and I would spend hours, during that visit, just talking, catching up on the lives of her three grown sons and my own son, to whom she is Godmother, but our initial greetings were brief. I was unashamedly anxious to meet the tall, brindle dog who stood quietly behind her in the livingroom, and I made no pretense of feeling otherwise.

Al Nice was, like most dogs, beautiful. I stroked the fine coat which covered the flatness of his back — typical of his breed — and felt the classic bones rising above and forward of his hips — bones which are expected to show in a well-fed greyhound. The touch of my hand stilled a natural quiver which seemed to begin in his cheek muscles and move backward and over his neck and shoulders each time he closed his muzzle and to stop when he opened his mouth in a pant. I smacked his hindquarters affectionately, and smiled at the way the hair grew into the characteristic bend of his long, skinny tail, near its tip.

The dog's ears, placed far back on his head, were one of his most obvious points of genetic specialization and really quite remarkable, in form and function. At rest, the ears fall into neatly folded triangles of soft velvet, pointing downward. While I admired them, a dog barked, outside somewhere, and the ears stood rigidly to listen, the creases of their folds disappearing. I found that I could manipulate the soft ears into their racing configuration — a thing the dog would do reflexively, as he started to run. Then they would hug the curve of his head, the soft points almost meeting at the back, a position in which they would offer almost no resistance to the air rushing past him as he ran.

The dog stood quietly, watching me with large, brown, liquid eyes. He accepted my examining him, and my admiring him, as he seemed to accept everything that happened with perfect discipline. When I asked if we could take him outside, he apparently understood the word, for he went to the kitchen door to wait for us. When Charlotte snapped a lead to the dog's collar and started through the door, he seemed to change gears as if, like a well-disciplined soldier, he came to attention.

The door led into Charlotte's cluttered garage and, immediately, we came upon a laundry basket which partially blocked our way. Although there was room for us to have walked around the basket, Al Nice, who was leading the way, came to an abrupt halt.

"There; that's what I was telling you about," declared my friend. "He could walk around that basket, but he just doesn't seem to have sense enough to know that. Isn't that exasperating?"

Now, as I said, Charlotte Iles has had dogs of one kind or another ever since I've known her, but she's always spoiled them, and now I suddenly saw through the dilemma over this facet of her dog's behavior.

"Charlotte!" I whispered, "Give him some slack and tell him to go."

Charlotte looked at me for only a second, then turned and gave a slight flick to the leash. "Go on, Al," she said quietly, and the dog sidestepped the basket and walked briskly forward, past Charlotte's blue truck, and out of the garage.

Charlotte stared at him, open-mouthed. "What happened?" she asked.

"It was a barrier," I told her. "He's been taught to stop, and to stay, at a barrier until he's given permission to go around it. He's not stupid; he's just the most well trained dog you've ever had."

And then we both stood there laughing at ourselves and each other and the amazing Al Nice, who stood watching us and commenting upon our discovery with a slight wag of his tail.

And that's when I realized another thing about this greyhound. He doesn't sit. He's doesn't seem configured to sit. He's configured to stand and to run, even to leap. When he's told to move, he moves; when he's not told to move, he stands still, like a soldier at parade rest.

Now, Charlotte removed the leash from the dog's collar and I saw him revert to what I decided to call his "loose dog" status. He came alive and ran about the yard, sniffing, snorting, investigating. He nuzzled Boss and, together, they disappeared around the corner of the house, loping easily.

When the two dogs returned, Charlotte waved a frisbee in the air and said, "Watch this." As Al Nice became alert and fixed the frisbee with an immovable eye, I remembered Audrey Alderson's telling me that a greyhound chases the cotton rabbit because it has been trained to follow an object it sees, not something it smells or hears.

Now, when the frisbee left my friend's hand and went sailing to the other side of the yard, a distance of some seventy feet, two things happened simultaneously. The first of these two things was that Al Nice went into forward motion. I didn't see him bend his hind legs and gather his strength in any sort of crouch and begin to move. He was just suddenly moving.

The second thing which happened in that blink of an eye was that Al Nice caught the frisbee. Clear over there, on the other side of the yard. In the same moment he left our side, it seemed, he was over there, catching the frisbee. I never saw anything like it.

Charlotte gave me the frisbee when Al Nice had brought it back to her, and I watched him, again and again, and it was always the same. His setting his body in motion was absolutely effortless; his burst of speed was phenomenal. His joy in running was complete.

Later, on a quiet road, I took Al Nice for a run. At least I ran, watching the dog as he loped effortlessly beside me. What a dog.

At bedtime, Charlotte humored me by placing Al Nice's blanket on the floor on the far side of the bed I would sleep in, and he curled there for the night. Just after daylight some small noise awakened me, and I opened my eyes to see the dog's face only inches from mine as he stood, chin resting on my pillow, watching me with those bottomless brown eyes.

In the days which followed, I would see in Al Nice the fine, even temperment, a gentleness amounting almost to thoughtfulness, and a quiet manner of deportment which would surely endear his kind to any owner. These traits, together with an undemanding nature and unquestioning loyalty and obedience, are typical of his breed. After earning an honest living as few dogs are allowed to do, they seem, in retirement, content to simply share the attributes of their good breeding and boundless affection with someone who will love and care for them.

No upstart in the canine world, the greyhound is an ancient breed. Great Britain, where it was first used to chase hares, is claimed as its country of origin but likenesses of dogs very similar to the modern racer are to be found on Egyptian tombs dating back 5000 years.

When I drove out of Aiken at the end of my visit, I knew that if I were to live again within a space which will accommodate a dog, I would adopt a retired racing greyhound.

THE WILLIAMS COW

Launching a Texas cattle business with one pregnant Brahma cow while doing justice to a whole other full-time job, might seem to mark a fellow as somewhat different from the usual run of ranchers, but Ralph Pitre had never bucked at being a different sort of individual.

The idea of having a ranch of his own went back as far as he could remember, and probably beyond memory, to the day before his second birthday, when he had first felt beneath him the movement of a roping horse — felt it from the safety of his grandpa's protecting arm, holding the little boy close against his chest. It was then, and on a lot more days like it, as the patient horse walked among Noah Pitre's placidly grazing herd, that Ralph had begun to hear from his grandpa the horse and cattle stories which would shape his grown-up life.

Before pursuing his dream, Ralph took the time to become a certified welder and worked the big rigs in the Gulf of Mexico, off the Louisiana and Texas coasts. He also acquired a wife, Jean, and two years later, a son they named Noah, after the grandfather who had been Ralph's teacher. Eventually, the dream beckoned and the welding business moved ashore.

Not long after that, Ralph bought the first pregnant cow. Then he bought another, and another. Acquiring cows which

120

were already in calf gave him an assurance of their fecundity, and fecundity was the first rule of building a herd. It also saved him the expense of buying a sire, for the kind of sire he had set his mind on would be beyond his financial means for some time.

He bought carefully, culled and sold carefully, and bartered his expertise with a welding torch for the service of a neighbor's fine, blooded Hereford bull. It was called herd management, and by the time he acquired The Williams Cow, he and his wife Jean, and the boy Noah, had managed the herd up to some twenty head of producing cows.

Each of the cows had a name, given for some special trait Ralph saw in her, and each member of the herd responded to the sound of his voice and even to the sound of his blue Dodge truck, bouncing through the pasture or along the road which bordered the pasture.

His latest acquisition was a little red-and-white Guernsey he'd bought from Joe Williams, a fellow rancher for whom he had a special liking and respect. For a while he referred to her simply as the cow he bought from Joe Williams. That was shortened, with use, to The Williams Cow, and that's the name she kept. There was no such hesitancy about naming her first calf, which earned its name right off the bat. But that's getting ahead of the story.

Ralph had bought the young Guernsey in late summer and trucked her home to his modest spread in a part of east Texas called the Big Thicket.

Reaching fifty miles north from the Gulf coastal lowlands, the Thicket covers a broad stretch of forests and prairies bordered on the east and west by two great rivers. Within these broad boundaries, twelve large, unconnected parcels of land have been set aside to be protected as the Big Thicket National Preserve. The isolated tracts not included in the

Preserve contain a half-dozen or so small villages and space for pastureland and private homesteads, like the one owned by the Pitres.

Jean and Noah had helped Ralph transfer The Williams Cow from the trailer to the fenced lot by the barn, and the three of them agreed on their high hopes for the little bovine's future, not as a herd cow, but as a provider of milk for their table. She was already scheduled to deliver her first calf in late spring.

Now, Little Thicket — the name Ralph and Jean had given their homestead — was bursting with springtime. In sight of the house, wildflowers had come to life on the rich, leaf-strewn woodsy floor, and a pileated woodpecker came daily to hammer at its favorite tree, renewing an old territorial claim. Bluejays swooped among the branches, shrieking, and a pair of Bewick's wrens had demonstrated their intention to build a nest under the hood of the Farmall tractor.

On an especially quiescent May morning, Ralph prepared to drive to Beaumont, some thirty miles away, on business. The last thing Jean said as he went out the door, was that he should bring a gallon of milk on his way home. He answered that, before long, they'd be getting their milk from the little Williams Cow.

Ralph revved the engine of the blue Dodge pickup to life, turned it around, and drove out of the yard, westward, through the trees that sheltered their home.

It had rained during the night, and the world was fresh and expectant. The oaks and pines and the floppy-leafed tallows were washed clean and green; high above the side of the road, the resident red-shouldered hawk sat on a powerline, watching for breakfast. In much the same primal manner, as he drove, Ralph glanced down each fire lane and fenceline right-of-way, checking, out of habit, for whitetail deer, knowing he probably would see none, as it was too early in the year and too late in the morning.

He slowed and shifted gears for the right-hand turn which, eventually, brought him out of the woods and into the open, circling toward the leased acreage where the herd was pastured. There, the Pensacola bahia, better known as poor man's grass, was long and sweet, alive with the song of redwings. Clumps of brushy myrtle, which grew in tall, scattered patches about the field, offered islands of quiet shade.

Ralph stopped the truck in the middle of the gravel road, idled it down, and released the gear. The Brahmas were gathered at the far end of the field. Three of the big gray cows, heavy with calves, had left the herd and were plodding slowly toward the high ground and the sanctuary of the brush.

"That's good; those old girls know what's happening," said Ralph to himself. As he sat watching his cattle, pride and a feeling of contentment worked his bronzed and bearded face into a grin. The Brahmas had been range bred for generations; their instincts for survival and their ability to cope with the laws of nature were deeply rooted, and their calving time gave him no cause for concern.

The little Guernsey, however, had been more gently bred. Her kind, accustomed to barns and close-in feedlots, might require some seeing to when the time came for the birth of her calf, now, probably, a couple of days away. The little red-and-white cow was standing with the grazing herd, showing no sign yet of seeking out solitude, as she would certainly do when the time for calving approached.

Everything was under control. Ralph mashed in the clutch, eased the truck into gear, and headed toward Beaumont.

123

* * * * *

It was considerably past time for his noon meal when Ralph Pitre started back from town, so he hurried out the Kountze highway and turned west, to pass through Sourlake. The land through which he traveled was open and sparsely populated, and he let his eyes roam to the horizon. He liked the open stretches of land. It was what had brought him to Texas in the first place, and it had been only the easy fall of circumstances which had caused him to settle in the Thicket, where he and Jean had found a good measure of contentment.

He turned right, just past the Hardin County School, and entered the tall trees. The red-tailed hawk, its morning hunt completed, had disappeared. Ralph's eyes scanned the beauty of the woods, his mind only momentarily mulling over the fact that the trees fenced in his view.

Driving into Saratoga, he toed in the clutch and geared down as he approached the grocery store. He pulled past the gas pumps and stopped long enough to pick up the gallon of milk and a tin box of Garrett's. The girl at the counter called, "Gotcha!" as Ralph held his purchases aloft for her benefit. He was outside, into the truck, and spurring it into a trot for home before she was finished writing his ticket.

Jean had heard the Dodge coming up the gravel road, and was standing in the yard, waiting for him. "Hey, girl, you needin' milk so bad you gotta be out here in the sun waitin' for it?" Ralph asked as he handed the plastic gallon jug over to her. "What you cookin' so special?"

But Jean looked worried. "Mister Carter just called," she told him. "He said when he went past, coming back from Liberty a while ago, he saw some buzzards over the pasture and thought you might want to check to see if we had any cows in trouble."

Ralph was back in the truck by the time Jean finished the sentence, thankful one more time for the wise presence of Alford Carter, an older cattleman with whom he had become friends.

Alford's farm lay near Kountze, a town nearly twelve miles away, but favors repaid in kind had made them neighbors in the old tradition of country living. Now, the man had taken time to let him know of possible trouble.

Ralph turned the truck around and drove out the driveway, kicking gravel as he headed back through the trees toward the turn-off which led to the pasture. He was damning the buzzards as he drove.

He was aware that buzzards — vultures, as the textbooks call them — are an asset in the country; they help keep roadkill cleaned up, for one thing. He also knew, as many of his grandpa's generation had not known, that when a vulture eats the carcass of a diseased animal — even a disease as bad as the dreaded cholera — something special in the bird's digestive system neutralizes the disease. Right this moment, he was reminding himself that vultures almost never killed healthy stock. But they can raise pure hell if an untended animal has trouble birthing in the open.

Since the very first time his Grandpa Pitre had shown him the buzzard-ravaged carcass of a just-born calf, Ralph had carried in his head a lifesize picture of a buzzard going for the eyes of its dying prey. The picture came to the surface of his thoughts now, and he pushed the toe of his dusty boot to the floor.

Coming out of the trees, Ralph scanned the sky, and saw no more than three or four of the big, black birds, their silver-tipped wings, a yard and a half across, flattened against the near heavens. He scanned the patches of myrtle brush and found nothing amiss. A small community of new Brahma calves lay beside their mothers among the myrtles, but they seemed safe enough.

The Williams Cow was not among them. Nor was she where he had last seen her, at the edge of the herd of Brahmas.

Then he saw the flock of vultures, gathered in a lone tree, near the center of the field. Oh, hell. There was the Guernsey, not more than fifty feet from them, in the open, and facing the forbidding black birds. The cow was down on one knee; he could tell by her belly, she'd had her calf, but he couldn't see it. He'd just bet the damn buzzards had killed it. Why couldn't she have had sense enough to go into the brush with the Brahmas before the calf was born. Dammit anyhow.

He stopped the truck, climbed out, and went to the fence. Standing on the top strand of wire and leaning on the steel fencepost, he could see the calf, splayed out near its mother, perfectly still, but no sign of any vultures, except those on the tree. There must be thirty of them sitting there, dressed like lean, hungry undertakers. If they'd already killed the calf, why weren't they finishing it off?

Ralph was thinking these things as he jumped from the fence on the run and pushed through the long grass toward the little Guernsey cow. He could see by now, she was almost spent.

Coming close, he clenched his teeth hard and a long sucked-in breath rasped through the tightened muscles of his throat, as he took in the scene of the cow's struggle.

Facing her tormentors, she held her ground in a ring of naked damp soil. The grass which had been in the ring was gone, trampled into the ground, and the ground was dug up as though it had been hoed. There, Ralph could see, she had circled and pawed and rushed at the birds, in defense of her calf.

126

Her legs were muddied to the knees, and spatters of the damp soil stuck to her sides and flanks, and mixed with the milk oozing from her swollen udder. Dirt smeared her face. Drying clumps of the stuff stuck to her forehead and to the swollen poll above it, showing how she'd used her natural talent for hooking, to throw dirt into the faces of her persecutors. Dirt was scattered where it had landed, in a broadening circle around the fortress she'd made for her baby.

The vultures, having harassed the little cow nearly to the point of exhaustion, were playing out the last phase of their game, waiting for their victim to stop moving.

The Guernsey was near collapse, but nothing about her said she was ready to give up. As the man came near, she straightened her front legs, rose, and turned to face this newest threat which was approaching her and her calf.

Tossing her head drunkenly, she lowed at him, her hoarse voice hardly an imitation of the bawling she must have done throughout the morning.

"Soooooo, girl. It's all right, little girl. Soooooooooo. Good girl. Good girl." Ralph talked quietly as he continued to walk toward her, slowly shaking his head as he thought about the battle she must have fought to keep the vultures at bay.

At last, she relaxed, tolerating his hand as he stroked her neck and sides. Still speaking softly, he patted her flank as he walked past her toward the calf.

The little body was stretched motionless in a yard-wide circle of fresh, untrampled grass in the middle of the torn-up ring of soil.

Without changing the tone of his voice or the words he was saying, Ralph knelt beside the still, small animal, amazed to find that only a single wound marred the soft red-and-white hide. On the calf's forehead, where a vulture had aimed for an eye and missed, a single wound was matted with dried blood. As he reached to stroke the calf's side, the long black lashes fluttered, and its eyelids rose over big, inky blue eyes.

The calf cried softly and, with a series of uncertain lurches, tried to stand, but Ralph held it down. The Guernsey, now up on all fours, seemed to be regaining strength, as she realized, somehow, that she no longer faced the danger alone.

"Come on, Little Buzzard; we've gotta get you and your mama out of the sun," Ralph said. He worked one arm under the small, velvet neck and the other around the calf's rump, and stood up, holding it close to his chest.

Then, continuing his soothing, one-sided conversation, he turned to walk toward the nearest clump of myrtle, and heard the Guernsey's soft footfalls following. When he placed her baby on the shaded grass, she began to lick it with her gentle gray tongue, smoothing its hair and removing the man scent.

The baby rose unsteadily beside its mother, then nosed its way to her udder as though it had done so a hundred times, found what it sought, and began to pull. As it gulped and the warm milk coursed down its slender throat, the small tassel of its tail began to twitch in healthy contentment.

Defeated, the patient black birds finally left the tree and flapped slowly skyward.

"Satan said to the Lord: 'Stretch out your hand and touch his bone and flesh, and see if he will not curse you to your face.

"Then the Lord said to Satan, 'So be it. He is in your hands; but spare his life.'"

From the Book of Job,
The New English Bible, Oxford Study Edition

JOB

Job

Part I

The Cat In The Yard

The sun had not yet climbed above the horizon when I
stepped out of my shoes and slipped quietly out the back
door. Shadows still obscured the deeply greened globe of the
orange tree, the gardenia bush, and low, secret places in the
butterfly garden. Bricks and concrete felt deliciously cool to
my naked feet as I walked toward the round glass table in a
corner of the patio. It was a comfortable time of day to enjoy
a last, unhurried cup of morning coffee, to watch the yard
come alive, and to consider how I would attack the day.

At the feeder, a brilliant cardinal kept a wary eye on his
surroundings as he deftly opened large striped sunflower
seeds, swallowing the kernels and discarding the hulls. High

overhead, in the pine tree, a gray squirrel sounded an alarm and, like the cardinal, I became instantly alert for some intruder.

I glanced about but saw nothing which might threaten any of the yard's usual inhabitants; it had been a long time since my own presence had seemed to make them fearful. I walked into the yard and looked up at the squirrel. Tail arched high as it chattered, the gray squirrel stared at the place where wild horsemint grew thick and high near the edge of the garden. There, huddled close to the ground, was a round gray form which, with a small movement, took shape as a large cat.

As the animal turned toward me, its eyes were the first detail I saw: enormous, yellow, alert, widely separated in a broad, gray face. On its forehead I could see the dark figure "M" which marked him as a domestic tabby.

"Hello, Baby," I ventured as, almost without thinking, I began to crouch, lowering my silhouette as I went slowly toward the cat.

His actions were baffling. The cat was unknown to me and must surely know he was in territory not his own, but he did not give ground as I approached; neither did he cower or offer any of the familiar warnings of aggressiveness. I paused as the cat broke our eye contact to look into the distance behind me, toward the place where the bowls for strays usually sat.

"Are you the fellow who has been making the supper scraps disappear?" I wondered aloud.

There had been times when I had heard the single syllable of a cat's "Now" in the night, but the unnamed dinner guest had always been out of sight by the time I turned on the light to look for it.

Now, as I drew nearer, palms turned upward and open, the gray cat returned my gaze and shifted his weight, as though to gather strength against the possibility of a need to run.

When I was almost within arm's reach, he rose to stand, sniffing the air. Perhaps something about the scent of the food bowl lingered there.

The cat had not waved his tail in greeting or flicked it as a warning to keep my distance and, considering this, I realized he had no tail. "What's happened to your tail?" I asked.

At the sound of my voice, the gray cat stood, warily, and I reached to place my hand on his broad head. Accepting my touch, he began to turn in a small circle, not leaving the spot in which he stood, but replacing step for step with his large, softly-furred feet.

His movement stopped abruptly as a breath caught in my throat. "Oh, no!" I cried, and the cat turned again to face me.

Quickly, I closed the distance between us and fell to my knees. I touched him gently, stroking his forehead and scratching briefly behind his ears. As my hand rested on his shoulders he drew a long, sighing breath and relaxed.

I turned him slowly, then, with the pressure of stroking him, and saw that not only was the big cat's tail gone, but the twin fleshy muscles which had once been his haunches, and the hide and hair which had covered them. All had been torn away by some terrible violence, leaving the ragged edges of flesh and bone, still damp with bright, not quite dry blood.

His eyes were fastened upon mine now, as though he might read my intention, and I tried to keep out of my voice the distress I was feeling as I said, "The sun will be so hot on that raw flesh, and it will get so cold when winter comes."

Then, I pleaded, "Lord, please heal him."

He tolerated my closeness and the pressure of my hands as I searched carefully for other wounds. Finding none, and giving his shoulder a last firm pat, I rose slowly to my feet.

"Now, you stay right here; I'll bring you a drink," I said, and walked away, toward the house.

I needed time to consider how this cat should be cared for. I thought about putting him into my own cats' wicker carrier and taking him to the animal hospital, a half-dozen blocks away, but decided against that. The anxiety of capture and confinement might be more harmful to him, just now, than to leave him be. The wound, though fresh, was no longer bleeding; he had cleaned it well. Furthermore, and perhaps most important, I wanted him to feel safe to return here to eat and drink, and to let me see to him if he needed care.

As water splashed into the bowl, I saw the cat lick his face and knew that, after his cleaning, he must be badly in need of water to erase the bloody, salty taste, and I hurried back to him with the water.

"There you are, Sweetie," I said, and placed the bowl on the ground in front of him.

The cat did not drink. Much as his dry throat must have ached and his swollen tongue must have longed for water, surely experience had taught him, as it has countless of his kind, that people do not usually give water or food or safe places. They give loud noises and thrown rocks and wounds that bring pain and make the blood flow.

My brief examination had shown me a tattered ear, a broken tooth, scars on his muzzle, all now well healed. These might be evidence of the price he had sometimes paid for the nearness of people.

The gray cat stood over the bowl without daring to look at the water but, unmoving, rolled his eyes to look at me through long lashes. Keeping my hands at my sides, fingers uncurled, so he would know I held no weapon, I turned and walked back to my now cold coffee, waiting on the table.

I watched as the tired, thirsty cat stood for a moment by

133

the bowl, then turned and walked to a nearby bush, where he raised a hind leg and sprayed, marking the territory for all to know as his own. Then, needing no one's permission, he returned to the bowl, now his by right of his own declaration.

He drank long and, looking refreshed and strangely elated, the cat circled the yard, pausing briefly to dampen first one place and then another, so there could be no question about the extent of his newly acquired territory. He uttered one quiet syllable which sounded like "Now," as he made his way out of the yard and disappeared among the empty vacation homes on the next street.

Having never seen the cat before in daylight, I was sure he would not return during the afternoon, but before dark I refilled the bowl with fresh water and placed it next to another containing the carefully provided leftovers of my supper table.

Later, when reading in the night, I heard the dull clink as the two pottery bowls touched and shortly, again, the small "Now," and then, quiet.

The cat did not return the next day, but again, before dark, I put out a meal for him.

* * * * *

The days and nights turned into weeks. The cat continued to come quietly in the night, to accept the cupboard love I provided, and leave behind the empty bowls. Sometimes I would hear the "Now," which I took for a thank you.

Summer was nearing its end when I was surprised one afternoon to hear the familiar "Now" outside the window on the shady side of the kitchen. I hurried down the steps to find the cat waiting for me, just around the corner of the house.

134

He neither flinched nor withdrew; he did not meow, or even come forward. He simply sat where he was and managed to look a bit detached, but not too detached.

"Hi, there. Are you hungry?" I asked. But the cat did not answer. I would have been surprised if he had. Cats of every description had been a part of my daily experience since childhood and I knew that, unless a cat is of the Siamese persuasion, or unless I am very well known to it, one will not often directly answer a direct question. Most often, when dealing with cats, one must do a good bit of assuming, about what a cat has in mind.

Now, I assumed the big gray tomcat was presenting himself in the expectation of receiving food or companionship, and I was prepared to give him both, in good measure.

I brought him food, but he did not eat. Instead, he came to where I knelt on the sidewalk, sniffed my hand, tucked his chin upon his neck and, leaning forward ever so slightly, rubbed a scarred ear against my knuckle.

Not daring to move in the surprise of this unexpected friendliness, I remained very still and talked to the cat, scratching the base of his ears, the hollows over his eyes, and the back of his neck, favorite itchy places of every feline. He circled on one foot as only a luxuriating cat can do, to rub his muzzle against the side of my hand, and what I saw as he turned brought a swift gasp, causing the cat to stop and look at me over his shoulder.

Hair! Hair on his haunches! Hair, where there had not even been hide or flesh to cover the bone. Hair, growing rich and thick and in perfect stripes to match the rest of his lovely coat.

"Oh, you dear, sweet cat!" The excited words were hardly spoken before I scooped him up into my arms — not even surprised that he allowed it — and carried him to the old green wooden chair in the corner of the porch.

Back and forth we rocked as I hugged him to me as though we were long lost friends — and he allowed that, too! More than that, he enjoyed it! Loud purring rattled up from somewhere in his middle, and he had his mouth open in a catsgrin, better to savor the smell of my hands and the traces of cooking which clung to them.

He purred and I rocked, pausing now and then to inspect the beautiful perfection of the hair which covered his haunches. Happy, wet tears rolled down my cheeks and darkened his fur as I held close to me the cat with the seemingly miraculous recovery.

Suddenly, his purring ceased and he wriggled from my arms. An unyielding aloofness took over as though someone had quite suddenly pointed out that, for a cat of the streets, he was being foolish.

He jumped lightly to the ground and, without a backward look, plodded to the gardenia bush, raised his leg and tinkled, and walked away.

His "Now," as he stalked across the yard, was a simple statement. "I hafta go somewhere," it said.

Or, maybe, it was "Thanks."

Or "See you later."

*　*　*　*　*

Part II

No Ordinary Cat

My inquiries in the neighborhood gleaned no information about the origins of the big gray tiger cat, though his movements were known for a several block radius of our quiet, suburban street.

Reaction to his presence ranged as broadly as his own wanderings and I knew, from having seen him while on my own daily walks, that he frequented a several blocks square parcel of county owned property not far from home.

I heard it said he killed kittens, but nothing I learned about him from my own experience added any weight to such a rumor.

Some said he was "purely mean", and was prone to seek out and attack resident housecats as they investigated the flowerbeds and dooryards of their owners. Others declared he was a quiet cat, seldom seen as more than a fleeting, sometimes ominous gray shadow. No one, as far as the talk went, had ever tried to tame him; yet, he exhibited traits usually seen only in a cat which has spent mutually pleasurable time with people.

He was a big cat, with a large, broad face and deep, expressive, golden eyes - windows barely shuttered and only suggestive of a deeper personality I would gradually come to know. Each foot had the addition of a "mitten" thumb, which made his paws extra large and gave him a plodding gait, as though he was always sure of his ground and deliberately bound for whatever was ahead.

Before long, and of his own volition, he formed the habit of coming regularly to eat and to be held, and to sit on a backyard table to be brushed and combed.

He made it obvious he had no intention of becoming my House Cat; quite the contrary, he never left room for the slightest doubt about his status as a beau of the streets. He possessed a high degree of the social graces and had about him always the air of a gentleman who preferred to live as he did, with no question of having been forced to it.

When he came for a visit, he made his way up the street, or between nearby homes, to arrive quietly at the back door. If I had not seen his approach, he sat politely, waiting to be noticed, or caught my eye by the very slightest movement and then looked aside, as though he hadn't really meant to stare. But as soon as I spoke to him, he answered my "hello" with the most genteel of one-syllable replies.

"Now?" he would ask, rising to greet me.

At mealtimes, the gray cat displayed the most polished of manners, accepting whatever food was offered and cleaning the bowl, when he was finished, with quiet laps of his tongue, just as a mother who had been a perfect lady, might have taught him.

Afterward, he often inclined his head and looked askance in a way I soon learned meant he would very much appreciate a lap to sit in. Somehow, there was always time to spend with this cat of the streets. Most often, we sat in the old green backyard chair for a time of rocking. I would tell him what a good and beautiful cat he was and he would respond with purrs of contentment and the gentlest of pawings upon my arm.

His throaty song seemed to come from the very depths of his heart and soul and to involve every part of him. It was an effortless offering, the beginning of which coincided with his settling into my lap or with the stroke of my hand upon his shoulder. Seldom did he sleep there; rather, it was as though a better spending of our time was in the discussion of the events of the day.

To end these lap sessions the cat simply ceased his loud purring, rose to his feet, and hopped lightly to the ground. Sometimes, if the weather was good, he stayed to sleep for awhile in the shade of the gardenia bush or, on cold or rainy days, on the small porch just outside the door. Usually, he stopped by the water bowl for a drink and then ambled away across the yard, uttering a small "Now," as he went.

On the rarest of occasions, he pawed at the screen door to make it known he wanted to come indoors. Inside, he checked things out, plodding through the rooms, sniffing at the usual lie-down places of Barney, the pampered Siamese. Returning to the kitchen, he helped himself to a meal from Barney's bowl. When he was finished he went to the door, and waited for it to be opened.

It was as though he felt compelled, from time to time, to make this brief tour of inspection. There was always an urgency about the visit, as though house calls weren't really quite the accepted activity for an independent outside cat who had important matters waiting elsewhere. His first visits inside made me apprehensive about his intentions and the extent of his good manners, but not once did he choose to mark an indoor area as his territory.

Evidence of the consistency of the cat's night life was to be found in his frequent injuries. From time to time I treated abscesses on his face and nose, a lacerated ear, claw or fang punctures on his paws and front legs, each wound a testimonial to his having faced another feline — whether amorously or in anger, I had no way of knowing. The cat was the soul of patience when treatment was necessary, and his wounds always healed in jig time regardless of their severity.

There was ample evidence that, in spite of the damage which was inflicted upon him from time to time, he enjoyed the good offices of some special feline guardian angel and, before long, the people who knew him began to call him The Lord's Cat.

The idea stemmed, at least in part, from the incident of the tapeworm. One day, as the gray cat left, after a curled-up nap on the mat outside the back door, I noticed, where he had slept, a broken segment of the flat, white parasite and realized the cat's intestine was infected. Early next morning, I went to Midway Animal Hospital and purchased the required antidote from the dispensary.

The cat chose that week to remain away for several days and, in the meantime, a widow up the street bemoaned to me the fact that her own cat had given evidence of the same ailment, and she didn't know how she'd work the price of a trip to the vet into her already groaning budget.

Reaching into the cupboard, I took down the envelope which contained the pills I had bought, and handed them over to my friend. "Here, take these," I said. "The Lord really seems to take better care of that gray tiger than I can, anyhow."

A week or so later, I took Barney for a routine visit to the clinic and, as Bill Bone, the veterinarian, was examining him, he said, "One of the girls told me you were in the clinic the other day for some worming medicine. Was it for Barney?"

"No, it was for the big gray tiger who's been coming around," I told him.

"Did you get him to take the tablets?"

"Uh, no; I gave them to another cat."

"Why don't you bring him in and let me look him over; he needs to get rid of those parasites," my friend counseled.

"Well, I think he'll be okay," I said.

More and more, I had become possessed of a feeling that my initial prayer for this cat had placed him under an umbrella of safety and that it was not I who continued to hold the umbrella over him. Now, with no idea at all of how this man of medicine might feel about such things, I was left to dawdle with words.

"I don't think he has them any more," I said. "Uh, I haven't seen any more evidence that he still has them."

Bill Bone may not have had the strictest faith in me as an instrument of the Lord, but he respected me as an owner and observer of the animals I brought to his clinic. "Are you sure it was a tapeworm you found on his bed?" he asked.

I told him I was.

"Well, cats don't get rid of tapeworm without treatment," he advised. "Next time you see him, bring him on in and I'll have a look."

Several mornings later when the cat came arching around my ankles, I groomed him, put him into the carrier, and took him to Midway. Bill took a feces sample from the cat and dispatched his assistant to the lab to make the test, while he gave the cat a thorough going over, pronounced him healthy, and administered the necessary injections to protect him against diseases of the streets.

Before long, Bill's assistant came into the examining room to announce, "Everything's fine. No tapeworm."

"Are you positive?" Bill asked.

"I surely am," said the girl.

Bill reached into the sterilizer for another loop-ended, stainless steel instrument, and proceeded to take another sample of the cat's feces. Behind him, the assistant rolled her eyes in mock exasperation and held out her hand to take the instrument. "Please run another test," Bill told her, and

141

handed her the specimen.

When she returned, she was grinning. "Well?" asked the vet.

"No parasites."

"You're sure?

"Positive," she said. "That cat's negative."

"Well, he must not have had a tapeworm in the first place," muttered Bill, as he stroked the cat's well furred, tailess rump. The usually entirely-with-it veterinarian presented a trace of unaccustomed absent mindedness as he placed the unresisting cat in the carrier and fastened the catch. "Keep an eye on him," was all he said as I picked up the carrier and turned to go.

I may have seemed a bit some-other-where myself, as I murmured my thanks and walked out the door.

At any rate, the gray tiger cat had an easy way of quickly putting troubles behind him and always displaying - at least, in our part of the neighborhood — a compatible disposition.

I had been casting about for a name for the big gray cat since the second time I had seen him, when it occurred to me than that, while he might never be wholly my cat, he might consider me his person. None that I thought of seemed really to fit him. Just as I knew this was no ordinary cat, I knew that no ordinary name would do. In spite of his transient lifestyle, names like "Hobo" or "Rover" denoted a silliness which did not suit his cavalier style. People names, like those I'd sometimes given to cats in the past, didn't seem just right, either.

I was at a loss about this until one day, after an absence of several days and nights, he came to the door and meowed with an unaccustomed urgency in his voice which demanded my attention. I found him peering through the screen door, scraggly, unkempt, and hungry looking. His fur had a decidedly ruffled look, and his countenance seemed, somehow, awry. While he ate from the hastily-filled bowl, I gathered brush, comb, flea spray, and a clean towel for rubbing him down.

When he finished eating he came to me, and I picked him up. Cradling him in my arms, the better to examine him for knicks and tears, I saw that a swollen abscess was pushing his poor nose all askew. I was filled with compassion for the long-suffering cat which seemed so often bedeviled by the ragged blows of life, and I hugged him to me. As I hugged him, I crooned.

"Poor, poor baby," I sang to him. "You've had every plague man and beast can put upon you. Your name should be Job."

From that moment, he was Job, and within twenty-four hours, he was answering to the name as though he'd known all along that it was his.

Part III

Job's Friends

Soon after Job settled into a routine of eating and, sometimes, sleeping in the vicinity of the back door, he began to bring with him a succession of presumably homeless and always hungry friends and acquaintances.

Job, I thought, was no more than two or three, four at the most, years old. The ages of his friends varied from kittens just old enough to be away from their mothers, to old down-on-their-luck cohorts, dredged up from among the local and, perhaps, the not-so-local cat populations. He shared his bowl with all of them, as though he knew that to do so would in no way diminish the size of his own meal.

A cross word, a threat, or a snarl was never heard between Job and any of the cats he brought to be fed. Sometimes, a stranger accompanied him to the food bowl for several days; sometimes, only once. For the most part, his friends were unclean, unkempt, and looked, certainly, unowned. I chose not to preach to them, however, about slovenly habits or their lack of responsibility, following, instead, Job's example of simple acceptance.

When he appeared, one day, with a skinny black female of markedly shy demeanor, I had no cause to think her any different from the others who had come and, in the course of things, gone, during the past months. This friend of Job's was slim, sleek, long-legged, long-tailed, a particular type of black cat which I have always admired, and with two of which I had once shared chapters of my life.

The affection and intelligence of such cats had ensured that any others of their breed would receive my warm welcome.

Now, this latest friend of Job's needed no other reference than her need and Job's silent recommendation to make her welcome and beloved. I could not imagine what past events had placed her in such fear of people that she would even leave a badly-needed meal in her dash for hiding and safety if I came near her. In the months which followed I spent many hours attempting, never with any complete success, to gain her confidence.

The first order of our acquaintance was to put some meat on her ribs for, when I first saw her, she was little more than a black shadow. Her delicate, wedge-shaped face was marred by two bare spots which I recognized as scars left by ticks. These, too, made the cat more precious as they indicated her lack of someone to care for her.

When the days grew frosty, as they sometimes do even in central Florida, I met her with morning bowls of warm oatmeal laced with meat scraps, cooked milk, and vitamin powder. Afternoons, she would quickly devour a bowl of Purina Cat Chow. She was never able to concentrate fully on her meal, but ate with one eye fixed warily upon her surroundings.

Just as I decided the healthful diet was bringing about a little rounding in the muscles of her shoulders and hind quarters, I was alarmed to discover that the roundness of her belly was gaining even more noticeably. It was obvious that Job was going to be a father. The black female could go not a moment longer without a name. Although there was no reason to believe her antecedents were anything but American or, perhaps, Oriental, I named her Mamacita, the lovely word the Spanish have for "little mother."

It was then I realized Job had hung about full-time for only a short while after bringing Mamacita to me. Then he had returned to his earlier habits, coming only for meals and to be cared for. Although I missed his presence, I realized we had contracted no formal agreement about time-sharing or the bestowal of permanent affections, and that to have his company at all was to have it strictly on his terms.

Part IV

Job's Kittens

Mamacita continued to come to the back door to be fed. With a daily portion of vitamin powder added to her regular meals, her ebony coat took on a rich sheen and she no longer had the hungry look I had first seen. Job paid her little heed, as he was away, most of the time, pursuing his carefree, bachelor ways.

The day came when Mamacita did not arrive to be fed, and I worried about whether she had found a safe place to bear her kittens.

When I was a child, woodsheds, barns, and open garages, hay mows and mangers and the quiet feed boxes of horses had provided snug nurseries for farm cats and their babies, but there were no such places available in the sterile, urban environment in which we lived.

Unwilling to accept the nearness of humans, Mamacita, I was sure, would have to make a bed for her kittens on the bare ground under one of summer's vacant homes. I wished for a better solution, but there was nothing I could do about it. She was, after all, an outdoor cat who continued to resist my every effort to tame her. Like Job, she probably qualified as "feral."

In due course, Mamacita returned from her confinement. Shed of her burden of babies, but consigned now to nursing them, she was again thin, hungry, and thirsty. She drank deeply, snatched a quick meal, and left. The stray cat part of my life was back to normal.

At last the morning came when I looked out to find a pair of tiny Job look-alikes playing on the patio. I was beside myself with excitement and, while I watched, a black kitten came running from under the house, followed by another gray tiger, another black and, last of all, a lovely all-over-gray kitten.

On hands and knees, I searched the farthest corners of the kitchen cupboards for a feeding pan which would accommodate the newcomers. A flat, nine-inch pottery baking dish proved just the ticket, its low sides reminiscent of the pans around which cats and kittens clustered to receive warm milk twice a day when I was a child.

Most of the new stock of cats and kittens in those years had come from friends and relatives who knew my weakness and most often "saved one for Mary Ellen" when litters were given away.

Welcomed as mousers on the farm, they grew and produced litters of their own to be bestowed upon friends and neighbors. Once, as Mother filled the catpan with warm, foaming milk she had just taken from a cow, thirteen cats meowed, stood on hind legs reaching toward the milk pail, and tangled themselves around her feet. It was then she presented the ultimatum that not another cat should be brought home until giveaways had pared the pack to a more manageable size. I was sure this group of Job's family and friends would never reach such a large pack.

I thought that, when the kittens were old enough to drink from the bowl, I would be able to pick them up and begin a new love affair with each of them. I hadn't been one-on-one with a litter of kittens in ages, and the prospect was exciting.

At the first sound of the opening door, however, Mamacita streaked toward the dark crawl space under the house, her kittens following as fast as their baby legs would allow, bumping into each other and tumbling over one another in their flight.

To my total dismay, these, and most of the kittens from her later litters, as long as they were unweaned and under Mamacita's tutelage, never accepted the closeness of people in spite of being brought to the door at an early age. Instead, they followed unerringly her rigid don't trust example. They came to the door to sit quietly, their presence all the voice they needed, to ask for food, racing into hiding when I answered. If one of the kits was slow in its retreat, Mamacita's snarl brought instant action.

Job seemed to take no part in the kittens' training. They often interrupted his naps in the sun to climb over him, bat his ears, and use his body as a hiding place from which to ambush one another. He tolerated this well, and treated them gently.

That Job had had a part in gendering these kittens, there was no doubt. In addition to being an extremely large cat, Job had other genetic traits which were not run-of-the-mill characteristics.

His large face was a flattish oval, rather than round or wedge-shaped. Seeing him for the first time, friends often compared him to a chipmunk, for his broad cheeks, at first glance, looked much like the pouches of a pocket rodent. The striped kittens bore a striking promise of developing this look.

It didn't take long to see that Job had passed on to the tiger kittens, the gene of his mitten thumb. The black kittens, and the one which was solid gray, did not share the inheritance.

There was no telling how far back I set the possibility of their taming when I whooped aloud my realization that these gray tiger kittens were, indeed, little Job-cats, for my excitement sent them scurrying away, to peer at me from dark safety under the house.

The black kittens were small images of their mother. I knew they would grow into lovely cats. In each litter Mamacita brought to us there were, in addition to the parent look-alikes, one or two kittens whose blue-gray fur was accented by liquid golden eyes. All of them were such darling little things, I had no doubts about their faring well when it came time for their adoption.

Mamacita brought us three similar litters during the time she was a part of our lives. Aware as I am that female cats, or queens, are not constrained to confine themselves to the service of a single tom when the mating season is upon them, the total similarity of all of these litters led me to believe they were of the same Job-and-Mamacita lineage.

As the kittens grew and were weaned, they would come to accept the touch of my hand and then grow accustomed to my fondling them.

Too soon, however, it would be time to find homes for them; those I did not place with friends would have to go to the Saint Petersburg SPCA. Though I cried all the way there and all the way home when it was time for their transport, the tears were not for the kittens as much as for myself, for the shelter had a fine reputation for placing both puppies and kittens, and I knew the people there would do their very best for my little charges.

If I were to relive the Job chapters of my life, I would have the dear big cat neutered to avoid the continuing production of kittens with Mamacita and with other lady cats he undoubtedly squired and serviced, but we cannot go about our lives filled with regret for what might have been or what we have not done. Suffice to say that, since Job, I have steadfastly supported the neutering of strays as a way of showing my affection for them.

Eventually, there was a time when I realized Mamacita

150

had not come to the food bowl for many days and I knew that I had seen the last of another of the cats in Job's life.

The fact that Job was here for a greater purpose, and that he served that purpose well, could never be doubted in the events which followed.

Part V

Job's Orphan

Thanksgiving house guests had departed and the family's routine was getting back to normal. The warm sunshine of what passes for autumn on the Florida Gulf coast flooded through open doors and windows. Walking into the kitchen one afternoon, I saw Job, sitting on the small porch, silently asking for attention.

"Hi, Job," I said, as I reached for the box of chow. I was about to start a one-sided conversation with the cat when my thought was interrupted by the flash of a tiny white kitten racing across the porch between Job and me.

As I gathered my suddenly scattered thoughts, I paused in disbelief, staring, first at the place where the kitten had been, and then back at Job. I had seen the kitten for only a moment, but a blurred suggestion of pale brown color about its face and ears made me wonder if it was Siamese.

I hurried outside to look, but there was no kitten in sight. Flattening myself to the ground, I peered between the bricks which formed a foundation around the back of the house, but I could see nothing of a kitten there, either.

"Joby, did you bring that kitten home?" I asked him, but the big cat only wrapped himself around my ankles and purred, perhaps more to encourage me to hurry with his dinner than in acknowledgment of my question.

I prepared his food and while he ate I watched, out of sight near the door. Job had finished his meal when the kitten crept cautiously into view. Sure enough, the first faint coffee-colored points of its Siamese background ringed the edges of the baby cat's ears, and vague brown shadows smudged its nose, paws, and tail.

I was totally mystified. Where in the world could Job have found a Siamese kitten and why had he brought it here? How had such a young kitten managed to become lost from its owner? However would I discover where it belonged? It never occurred to me that such a tiny bit of catlife might have no home, no parents, and no people.

When the kitten had finished its meal, Job washed its face and shouldered it back under the house. I did not see it again that day.

The next morning when Job came at breakfast time to be fed, I filled the bowl and put it down for him and stayed only long enough to ask again the about the origins of the kitten.

Returning to the kitchen, I paused out of sight to watch and almost immediately the tiny white kitten ran from hiding to join Job as he ate. The big cat had once again brought "company" to share his own good fortune. As soon as the kitten had eaten, however, it disappeared again under the house.

Later in the morning, I took a pan of pole beans to a seat on the patio and began to snap them for cooking. I was sure the kitten was still under the house, and I wanted to give myself every opportunity of seeing it.

I had been working quietly for some time when the tiny creature appeared, ran around the corner of the house, and disappeared. It had a strange, uneven manner of walking, seeming to favor its left hind leg, which I could not see. Following it, I found small spots of fresh blood on the concrete where the baby cat had climbed over a brick to return to its sanctuary under the house.

A short while later, it reappeared, running in the opposite

direction, and what I saw brought a gasp of disbelief into my throat. Its tiny left hind leg ended just above the place where the heel joint should have been. It was from this severed stump that blood was oozing to mark the pavement with each step the kitten made.

The questions came flooding back, with new ones added now to the mystery. How had this little creature been so injured, and why was it not being cared for? Surely, the kitten's mother must have been owned. Why had no one come looking for it?

Remembering the terrible wounding which had recently happened to Job when he had first appeared in my yard, I was not really puzzled by his bringing the kitten home to me. The possibility that he had brought it to be cared for, as he had been, placed me deeper in awe and wonder of the minds of all animals and, in particular, of the uncommon cat I called Job.

It soon became clear the kitten felt safe in the open only when Job was present. She deferred to him as she would have to her mother, and Job performed admirably in the role of a single parent. He tolerated her tumbling over him and gnawing at his ears and tail. He shared meals with his little charge, bathed her as her mother might have done, and the two spent long hours curled together on the warm sunny concrete. The churring voice he used to call her from her hiding place was totally unlike the "Now" he used to attract my notice or to acknowledge my gifts of food or care.

Occasionally, I watched the pair as they made their way across the yard on some errand. Job, head high, marched in the lead and the kitten, in spite of her pitiable limp, capered along in his shadow. Together, they would spend long hours away, I knew not where, always returning at suppertime to eat and spend the night under the house.

Then, that, too, changed.

November was past, and the early days of December were putting themselves behind us.

Never tiring of the sight of cats just being cats, I stood watching, one morning, as they finished breakfast and washed their hands and faces. I yearned to gather up the hapless kitten, to bathe her and brush the soft, creamy fur which I was sure lay beneath the covering of grime. But more than anything else, I wanted to begin to convince her that the entire world was not a fearsome place.

When they had finished bathing, Job walked across the patio as if to leave, and the kitten followed. At the edge of the concrete, the big cat paused and stood perfectly still.

The kitten stopped, and Job moved on.

The kitten ran to him and, again, Job stopped. He turned to stand broadside and stiff-legged in front of the kitten. He did not turn his head, but only rolled his eyes in the kitten's direction.

It was a long moment before the big tomcat turned to move across the grass and once more, the kitten ran to his side. He stopped, whirled toward her, and some sort of communication passed between him and the little cat.

Suddenly, I was a child again, running after my father as he went toward the automobile waiting in the driveway. I was pleading to go along to wherever it was he was going that morning, but his stern, "Not this time" had an air of finality not to be argued with. The way I had felt then was the way the kitten looked at this moment: rejected, lonely, and sad.

She crouched submissively, looking up at her protector. When he did not move, she began, very slowly, to rise again, as though to test the gray cat's resolve.

Job turned toward the kitten and shouldered her back to the patio, sat down beside her for a moment or two, and turned again, to walk away.

The kitten cried aloud, but did not move from where she sat. Job answered with a low, throaty churr, walked across the yard, and disappeared into the warren of homes.

Long after Job was out of sight that morning, the lonely little Siamese sat looking toward the place where he had disappeared. Finally she made her way back to the shadowed, safe place under the house.

The kitten continued to enjoy Job's company around the back door, but never again did I see her follow him out of the yard. It was as though he had made her understand that this was home now; she was to follow him no longer.

Neither did she begin to show any confidence in me as a replacement for Job, as I had hoped she would.

* * * * *

Word traveled fast of the little girlcat Job had brought home and which was staying under our house.

Florence Coto, who lived in a mobile home park which abutted our back property line, soon collected the pieces of the unfortunate kitten's story.

I had known for some time that the owner of the park Florence lived in was one of that strange sort who hate cats and that he had laid down a firm NO CATS rule for his homeowners and tenants. From time to time, the man's grandson came to hang around Florence's door and to warn her of what his grandpa would do if he ever saw her cat in the yard. Florence, a confirmed cat person who was known to champion the cause of cats in general, scorned the landlord's rule and kept a cat of her own.

Sage, an arrogant gray Persian, daily took the air at the end of a trailing cotton cord which was fastened, at its other

156

end, to a chair on Florence's porch. "She doesn't know she could break that string in a minute if she tried," Florence told me. "I started putting her on it when she was a kitten, and she's just never tried to get away from it."

It was Florence who had brought me the early tales of Job's untrustworthiness, tales which had been told her by other tenants in her park. But, scoffing at such gossip, Florence had staunchly defended Job, maintaining that he had never offered the least interference with Sage's peace of mind as she sunned at the end of her cotton string.

"Maybe he thinks the Persian princess is above his serious notice," I ventured.

Florence grinned and said, "More likely she's told him about her operation."

The kitten's story had begun when someone in Florence's mobile home park had told the landlord about the birth of kittens to a Siamese cat belonging to one of his tenants. The mother cat had made her nest in the semidarkness under a vacant mobile home where her babies were safe as long as they were infants. Their hiding place became evident, however, when they grew old enough to run about in the yard and to make noise.

The cat-hater, informed of their whereabouts, had killed the mother and two of the babies. A third little white kitten, so the story went, had escaped.

The second part of the tale Florence heard was that the hungry orphan kitten had been lured, with food, into the screened porch of a family who thought to keep her.

"They thought that was all there was to it," Florence said, in disgust, "and after she ate, they tried to pick her up, but she was so terrified, she just cried and tried to get away. She got under a roll-away bed that was stored in the corner, and the little boys beat on the metal frame with a broomstick."

157

Florence Coto was obviously aghast at the story she had to tell. "Can you imagine how scared that poor little thing was?"

After that, she said, the boys had decided they wanted nothing more to do with the wild little thing, and chased her outside with the broom.

No one remembered having seen the kitten for some time then, until, one morning, one of the tenants, out for a bicycle ride, heard cries near the steps of a vacant house. Investigating, she found the little cat, emaciated, cringing in terror, one of her hind legs hopelessly tangled in a rotting fiber doormat which had been discarded under the edge of the house.

While the tiny kitten cried in fright and pain, and struggled to be free, the woman tried to tear the fibers loose from the torn and bleeding flesh of its leg. Unsuccessful, she rode home for scissors to cut away the mat.

As the would-be rescurer had sawed at the doormat's tough fibers with her scissors, the kitten offered no defense, but simply howled and tried frantically to get free. The woman knew from the extent of its wound that the kitten must have lost a lot of blood. It was dirty and so starved looking, it hardly seemed worth saving. Probably the best thing to do, she had thought, would be to take it to the animal shelter and have it put to sleep.

She had nearly cut through the last of its bonds when the frightened little creature, with a cry of pain, struggled from her grasp and ran. Behind it trailed the remains of its left hind foot, a grisly mess of torn flesh and severed bone, hanging by threads of hide and tissue.

After that encounter, Florence Coto said, the kitten had not been seen again until Job appeared with her at my door.

As the kitten's story came to me in bits and pieces, I no longer wondered at the fright which kept it in hiding under the house, but I was determined to help it if I could and was willing to wait if I must.

Part VI

The Adoption

Christmas was almost here. The kitten had been living under the house for the better part of a month and I had never held it. I had never even come near touching it, and I felt surely, for me, that must be some kind of a record.

I had managed, once, to quietly poke a camera outside the door to snap a picture of the kitten and Job at the food bowl, but at the first sound of my presence, it had scurried under the house and stayed there until all was clear.

As the weather became cold, I prepared warm breakfasts of oatmeal, enriched with vitamins and the previous night's dinner scraps, just as I had done so often for Mamacita and her babies. These were followed by generous meals of chow in the late afternoons, and the kitten soon began to look plump and healthy.

Long before daylight, on the day before Christmas, as I sat reading near the living-room door, I heard outside, Job's single syllable of greeting, "Now."

I turned on the outside light and opened the door. Job stood on the porch, looking up at me. On the step below him sat the kitten. It was the first time I had seen her at the front door, and I had the feeling something special was about to happen. Much as I wanted to bring the kitten close to me, I thrust the anxious thoughts aside and kept my voice calm.

"Are you ready for breakfast, Joby?" I asked. "Come to the back door and I'll bring it out."

I went to the kitchen and drew aside the curtain which

160

covered the glass door. As I prepared the bowl of food, Job and the kitten arrived outside the door. This, too, was something new. Never before had the kitten appeared until the food was in place and I was back inside the house.

Now, when I took the food outside, the kitten hurried to the bowl and began to eat, while Job sat stoically at the foot of the steps. There was no doubt about it; the time was right.

I gently picked up the kitten and held her close, scarcely able to contain the warm and happy feeling which rose in my chest.

Job went to the bowl and began to eat, while I walked into the house with the little orphan cat.

Once inside, separated from Job for the first time, the kitten showed her disquiet by little nervous-seeming laps of her tongue. I talked to her soothingly, stroking her soiled fur and holding her close. When she seemed to be settling down, I took from the cupboard a box of Meow Mix which sometimes served as Barney's treats. Pouring some into a bowl, I sat down at the kitchen table, with the kitten in my lap. One by one, I took the tiny colored cat biscuits from the bowl, placed them in the palm of my hand, and watched the hungry kitten gobble them up.

She purred loudly as she ate, and I wondered if it was her equivalent of whistling in the dark, or if she was truly content to sit in my lap and eat. Or if the purring was an automatic thing which had nothing to do with me or what I was doing.

When she had eaten all she wanted, I simply sat there, stroking her, gently scratching behind her ears, and talking to her. She neither cried nor struggled to be free, but sat very still in my lap, and continued the loud, deep purring.

Street urchin that she was, her fur was filthy dirty, and alive with fleas. Under the dull, grimy coat were crusty sores, the result of her attempts to scratch away the vermin. The stump of her left hind leg ended just above the place where the heel joint should have been; the severed flesh, still seeping blood, was beginning to heal around the edges of the naked bone.

Her sweet little face was that of a classic doll-kitten, her big, round eyes the bluest I had ever seen; her whiskers and eyelashes were dark and luxuriant. Her fur seemed longer and thicker than other Siamese I had known and, grimy as it was, its quality was hard to discern.

Barney came to inspect the new kitten. As he stood upon his hind legs and reached to sniff at the little creature, he exhibited only curiosity and none of the vaguely hostile attitude he had shown newcomers in the past. For the kitten's part, she lay very still and allowed his inquiring nose to poke about upon her fur, her face, and the raw sore which was the ending of her left rear leg.

Using a gentle shampoo, I bathed the kitten, dried her with a soft, warm towel, and made her a bed near a bathroom warm air vent. Placing her upon it, I turned out the light, went out, and closed the door.

I was not surprised to find I could not leave the kitten alone and, periodically, during what remained of that night, I quietly opened the door to look in at her sleeping quietly. When daylight came, I prepared breakfast for the two cats, brought the kitten into the kitchen, and sat down to watch them eat. Surprisingly, Barney did likewise, relinquishing the bowl to her and eating only when she had finished.

When she had eaten her fill, she hurried from the bowl and, making a quick circuit of the kitchen, scampered into the small space between the wall and a huge, heavy old cupboard we called the monster. There she hid until mid-morning, when I heard Job's soft "Now," and found him at the back door, waiting to come in. Inside, he stood in the middle of the

162

kitchen, churring loudly.

Immediately, the kitten came from her hiding place and ran to Job. He greeted her with a quick licking of her face, and she wrapped herself around his legs, purring.

Job plodded into the livingroom, with the kitten following close behind. He jumped upon the sofa, a liberty he had never before taken for himself, and she climbed up after him. He gave her a complete bath, as a mother cat would have done, and they curled up together for a nap.

While they slept, I stuffed wadded newspaper into the place by the cupboard where she had hidden, and went back to my preparations for Christmas, which was the next day.

When the two awoke and came into the kitchen, Job ate from Barney's bowl, helped himself to a drink of water, licked the kitten's face briefly, and went to the sliding glass door, wanting to be let out.

The kitten tried to follow, but I closed the door, keeping her inside. She stood watching the big, tail-less gray cat as he crossed the porch, and then the yard, and disappeared.

Late in the afternoon, while we sat with guests over coffee and fruitcake in the kitchen, Job came to the back door, asking "Now?".

I let him into the house, and he went immediately to the living-room door. From there, he called the kitten from her new hiding place among the inner workings of my husband, Bud's, recliner chair. He washed her face and they ate together, and I took the two of them into my lap for awhile. When Job jumped down and asked to go outside, the kitten again followed him to the door, then stood arching her back and rubbing her face upon the glass until she could no longer see him.

Thai and Job

Early the next morning, Job once again came in to look for the kitten, which was curled up, asleep, in the underworks of the recliner. He went to the living-room door, stopped, sniffed, and took several steps toward the chair. For a long moment he stood, looking toward the place where the kitten slept. Then, apparently satisfied with what he had learned, he turned and walked deliberately to the back door, where he waited for me to open it.

Mystified by this drama which had unfolded before me over the past two days, I picked Job up and hugged him, but he squirmed to be put down, so I opened the door and he leaped from my arms. Without a backward look, he crossed the patio and walked quickly between the nearby houses as though he were late for an appointment.

After that day, Job continued to come to the door and sit patiently, waiting to be seen, as a signal that he wanted food or water or attention, but never again, during the remainder of his life, did he ask to come inside. When she saw him outside, the kitten scurried to the door and rubbed her face and the side of her body against the glass, silently begging him to notice her, but her appeals were steadfastly ignored.

It seemed that, as far as Job was concerned, he had done his part in the kitten's upbringing and now it was time to turn her over to someone he had learned to trust; someone, perhaps, whom he had come to have affection for, to whatever extent a confirmed bachelor feral cat is able to do that.

Part VII

Job's Legacy

I considered and put aside half a dozen names for the little cat and, at last, with a nod to the country of the origin of her breed, named her Thai (Tie).

On the day after Christmas, I took her to see our good friend and long-time veterinarian, Bill Bone. She sat quietly while Bill examined her wound, looked her over thoroughly, and administered her "baby shots." As he lightly massaged the needle site between her shoulders, he said, "She hasn't an aggressive bone in her body."

Bill's observation was prophetic, for Thai was never heard to utter a cry in anger. She never hissed or spat, or even slapped, as most every cat, now and then, does. Of course, she had no real reason to do any of those things, for she did not earn the scoldings, the cries of "No! No!" and "Get down!" so common among other cats. Quite the contrary, she was always a perfect model of sweetness: a gentle, well-bred little cat.

Thai stopped growing before she was a year old. Her small size seemed to intensify her dependency upon us and we thought of her and spoke of her, always, as a child cat.

Many of the natural tendencies of kittenhood seemed to have been subverted by the pain and terror of her early life. While she always seemed ravenous at mealtime and ate every treat offered in between, for many years she accepted only what was offered, asking for nothing more, nothing different, for she never once uttered a single meow until some time after

166

she had passed her sixth Christmas.

We offered her every kind of small cat toy we could find, but not even those filled with fresh catnip could lure her out of what seemed like a fear of being caught in the open with her guard down. When I picked her up, she purred and cuddled but even then, she seemed most content when she hid her face in the curve of my arm or under my chin. For a very long time, her only play was an occasional, brief game of ambush and attack with her good companion, Barney.

She seemed to want nothing more than to live a quiet, lonely existence, most often hiding if there were more than Bud and I in the house, and running in terror from such things as a car coming into the driveway or an unexpected knock on the door.

Bud was totally captivated by her from the first day she came to live with us, and I am sure he never raised his voice to her above one of kindness. Still, it was a very long time before she came to accept that she was safe in his presence and would tolerate his approach.

Although, from the very first, she seemed to enjoy my holding and petting her, Thai was nearly two years old before she made any overtures of friendship on her own. Quite suddenly one day, as though there had never been any reason for hesitation in the first place, she ran across the room and leaped into my lap, settled down, and began the loud purring which was so much like that of her mentor, Job.

From the moment of that first leap, my lap was hers, and Barney was unquestionably subject to dispossession any time he might have settled there first. She would accomplish this, not by any show of force, but by a slow and careful insinuation of herself into my lap. From that day, also, her favorite sleeping place was in the crook of my arm, head resting on the inside of my elbow or on my palm.

Sometime between her fifth and sixth year, she began to meow softly from time to time, but not until she was nearly ten years old did she put forth any real effort to make herself heard. It seemed she was beginning to accept us and, for a long time, we were surprised and felt especially honored when she uttered any cry at all.

At first, her talking was no more than a single brief "Mow?" when I entered the room where she was, or when I called to her. Then, as though she learned to like the sound of her voice, she rapidly developed a true Siamese vocabulary of long glissandos, trilling crescendos, and chortles. With a low churring noise, she threatened tiny lizards on the porch, and birds or squirrels or rabbits which came upon her lawn — all of this, of course, from safely behind a closed door or window.

As she grew older, Thai learned to carry on great conversations. Sometimes I talked to her in my own native English, sometimes in made-up meow words which imitated or even made fun of her own. She answered, assuming a broad variation of inflection and tone and, in turn, seemed to make inquiries of her own. Indeed, it was often Thai who initiated this great source of enjoyment for the two of us, so much more remarkable because of her long years of silence. Oh, how I wondered, as we carried on our indecipherable conversations, what the exchange might mean to her.

In her twelfth year, she quite unexpectedly learned to play. I would find her in an upside-down position, kicking and pawing in mock battle with the underside of a low chair in the living room. When she sensed my presence, she stopped immediately, as though remembering her dignity. She progressed to batting about a small ball of yarn which I left where she might find it, and when she accepted a tiny fur-covered mouse as a regular plaything, we were as excited as if a child had brought forth its first tooth.

Even though, for a very long time, she would not look into the face of a stranger, I could not resist the temptation to bring her from hiding to show her off. At those times, she would tightly circle my neck with both her arms, burying her face under my chin.

Her wound healed well, the unfurred stump forever reminding us of all she had endured and all that we, somehow, wanted to make up for. During one of her visits to his clinic, Bill Bone examined the well healed stump of her leg and wondered aloud if perhaps Job had been responsible for the neat and necessary task of finishing the amputation.

When Thai blossomed with the luscious hues of a true Sealpoint Siamese, I marveled that the coffee colored fur on the amputated leg grew above its customary height in a trick of optical illusion which made the two hind legs appear more nearly the same size, the missing foot and ankle less obvious. It was as though even nature herself wanted to make up, in some way, for the terrible accident which had occurred to Thai in her babyhood.

Ordinarily, when Bud and I have been away from home we have taken our cats with us, or close friends have provided for their care during our absence. When we planned a two weeks' trip to England, however, we decided to leave Barney and Thai with Bruce Hague, who has operated a grooming and boarding service next door to Midway's clinic for many years.

At that time, although Thai had been a member of our family for six years and at least an annual visitor to the clinic next door, Bruce had never seen her. On the day before our departure, I put Barney and Thai into their carrying baskets and went to turn them over to him. Plying me with questions, Bruce completed the forms which were necessary before he would accept responsibility for the two cats. Noting that they were both Sealpoint Siamese, he wanted to know how we told them apart.

"Well, their faces are very different; they're just different little people," I said, rather lamely.

"You know that," he said. "How will I tell them apart?"

"Barney is taller; Thai's fur is fluffier," I told him, wondering to myself, how different, really, two Siamese cats can be.

"I guess I can go with that," Bruce said, as he removed Barney from his carrier and took him, squalling, into the boarding quarters. While he was gone, I lifted Thai from her wicker basket, placed her on the counter, and was cooing to her when Bruce returned.

As he picked her up, his eyes widened and he looked at me in disbelief. "What happened to her foot?" he asked.

"She lost it in an accident, when she was a baby," I told him.

"Uh...." He studied Thai's leg, then looked again at me, and grinned. "That would be a pretty good way to tell them apart," he said.

For me, it seemed to put a stamp of finality on the fact that, although Bud and I now and then talked about all the worldly things we would be willing to part with, or endure if, by so doing, we could bring about the replacement of Thai's lost foot, we had ceased to think of her as "disabled" or physically different from other cats. This, in spite of the fact that when walking, she always limped noticeably. The limp, however, disappeared completely when she chased Barney through the house.

We never ceased to marvel at the ability of this small bit of cream and coffee fur and blue eyes to bring us happiness, and only when friends and relatives tell us of the extraordinary behavior of their own animals, do we have any hint of doubt that Thai was the most extraordinary little cat that ever was.

* * * *

When Barney was 11 years old, Bill Bone detected a serious irregularity in his pupils and set up a consultation with a feline ophthalmologist, Dr. Craig Fischer. Dr. Fisher confirmed Bill's diagnosis of a progressive ailment which would ultimately render Barney sightless.

In the years which followed, Barney did, indeed, gradually lose his sight but, as both veterinarians had led us to expect, he adjusted to his condition to a degree which prevented most visitors from realizing his disability.

As he grew old, and became unsteady upon his feet, he still came to be taken into my lap now and then, but gave up the old habit of snuggling at my feet at bedtime. He was willing to simply spend his nights on a soft rug in front of the refrigerator, made comfortable by its warm exhaust.

One night, during the first week of June, the week of his twenty-first birthday, he came in the night, nosed his way into the circle of my arm, and curled himself to sleep, purring in his familiar, quiet, contented way.

The next day, I knew Barney's time had come, and Bud and I went with him for his final visit to Midway.

There, the last things Barney knew were the ministrations of a caring circle of friends and the touch of my hands stroking his face as I whispered, "I love you," over and over again.

As for Job, although he never again acknowledged Thai's

171

longing for him or even her presence, after the Christmas Eve adoption, he continued as my beloved outdoor friend for several years. Then, like many outside cats who are exposed to all sorts of illness and disease beyond those against which they can be vaccinated, Job's health began to decline and, with a great deal of sadness, I gave him over, one day, to a quick and painless passing.

There had been absolutely no guessing at the poignancy of the events which would occur as a result of Job's first appearance in the yard and his decision to let me be his person. If ever the qualities of caring, dignity, perhaps even love, may be said to be a part of any cat's being, they must certainly have belonged to Job, an unforgettable legacy unequaled by any of the animals I have known.

Thai's behavior altered when she became an only cat. She was less apt to claim our attentions, as though she realized there was no longer a necessity to compete. She talked more than previously, and, quite unexpectedly, began what I chose to call her singing lessons. As though making up for the loss of Barney's loud, long, many splendored renditions of the Siamese ballads with which he had entertained us, Thai became a soloist.

Barney and Thai

172

Dr. William Bone retired from his practice, and new, loving caregivers came to Midway Animal Hospital. In late summer, three months before her eighteenth birthday, I looked through tears at an X-ray negative as Dr. Gwenneth Hall, one of the new veterinarians at Midway, pointed out a dark shadow on a picture of the little cat's lower jaw and said that it was cancer. Death might come, she said, in less than a month.

"Is there nothing we can do?" I asked.

With great kindness, Gwenn said, "Take her home and spoil her."

During the next several weeks, Thai had some good days, when it was almost possible to forget she was slipping away from us. Some of those times, as well as the not-so-good times, are recorded in my journal:

"Thai gets whatever she wants to eat. I open the things she has always liked best and simply throw away what she doesn't want."

"Today I cut some grass very fine for Thai. She loved it. It's as though she's spoiling us. She comes to sleep with me, as she used to, climbing quietly into bed, but waking me with her loud purring."

"This was a bad day for Thai. Looking back, it must have been a day of pain. I didn't see her do it, but she bothered her right hand until she took some of the hair off a small spot. I cuddled on the floor with her for a long time at bedtime. The three bunnies came to play on the front lawn and broke the awful spell of grief."

"Up in the middle of the night last night. Fed Thai and

cuddled her. Back to bed. Slept til 0700. Jackie Williams came, about noon, with flowers, books, M&Ms, and loving kindness. I told her I feel like I'm preparing to send Thai on a long journey alone. Jackie said that's because of her disability. I feel she needs me and I can't be there."

"Thai is losing ground; the growth is going inward. Tonight she has a frown. She sits with Bud and follows my every movement. Is she storing memories, as I am?"

"This morning, I opened a can of Swanson's chicken and shredded a couple of spoonfuls. Thai drank all of the can's broth, but ate no meat. Dear little love. It was time. We took her, together, to the clinic. All of the girls came in to tell her goodbye. She died with her little head where she liked it best, in the palm of my hand. Is she, really, with Barney and Job in the meadows of heaven? Will I find them, some day, waiting there, at the rainbow bridge?"

A few days later, I wrote: "It is amazing how prepared we seem to have been for Thai's going. There are cuddle times when I miss her awfully and cry. But if she had to go, the time was right and I'd done so much grieving already. Still, it seems impossible we have been diminished by only one small cat. There is life in this house only where we are, with no childcat to anticipate in a doorway."

By no means, however, was it the end of grief. A great sadness overtakes me at the strangest times. To drive it away, I think about Job, the Lord's cat, who had a purpose in his life and brought me a gift more precious than even I, who have loved cats all of my life, could have imagined a little cat could be.

WORKING DOGS

The first task a dog performed for a man, an act by which he acknowledged man as his master, was, in all likelihood, a spontaneous act on the part of the beast and came as a total surprise to the man. It would be interesting to know what that deed was, but there's no record of it.

What we know as Civilization was still many centuries away when the wild dog left its natural wandering lifestyle to become a part of man's family: to share his company, his food, and the warmth of his fire. The number of ways dogs have chosen to requite man for these comforts are legion; the pleasure and surprise this once wild creature invokes in its people seem to have no limit.

By the 1930s and '40s, when I was growing up on a Midwestern farm, a farmer expected to have a dog on the place.

Most often, the farmer's dog wasn't acquired as a working animal; it was valued simply as a companion who hurried to meet the family car when it came into the driveway, no matter how brief the master's absence had been. The dog romped with the farmer's children, and kept him company when a day's fence mending at the back of the farm might, otherwise, have been a lonely job.

Such an animal was considered to be a good watchdog if it roused the family with barking when strangers approached the back porch or the henhouse. And the dog might be traded off to a friend who had no close neighbors, if it was considered a "barker" who didn't know when to quit.

Most farm dogs were expected to be good ratters, for the prudent farmer was hesitant to put out poison to keep his barns and grainaries free of rodents. Setting traps was an unsatisfactory alternative, for the farmer's cats might be caught and a good mouser lost in the bargain.

Lonnie Powell, who lived with his family on a farm near our own, had a black-and-white dog named Jack, who killed rats, warned of intruders, and was a companion to Lonnie's and Carrie's six children.

When we drove there, in our ancient black sedan for a visit, we knew Jack would meet us halfway up the Powell's long driveway, escort us to a parking place in the dooryard, and greet us with a proper tail-wagging as we climbed down from the car. And he would see us out to the road again when our visit was finished. When he was told to, Jack trotted good naturedly into the pasture, rounded up the farm's herd of cows, and brought them to the barn for milking.

Like many other farm dogs, Jack was taken largely for granted. Nobody ever tried to figure out what there might be in his heritage which would explain his willingness and ability to work. His kind were simply referred to as shepherd-dogs or part-shepherd, and the subspecies description ended there.

Jack and other dogs of his ilk, acquired as companions, seemed simply to take on jobs which needed doing. For the most part, they did their work well and for no more reward than regular meals, a dry place to sleep and, sometimes, the enthusiastic praise of their people. They were almost never given the benefit of any formal training; their helpfulness came from natural instinct and a desire to please; and they seldom reached their full potential as working dogs.

I was probably nine or ten years old, and our farm had been without a dog for the better part of a year, when I arrived home from school one afternoon to find my Dad waiting for me by the kitchen door. "What's a-matter?" I asked, for I could tell something was in the wind.

"You want to get your clothes changed and go look in the barn floor," he said.

In those days, it never bothered me that my Dad was forever telling me I wanted or didn't want to do something. "Now, you don't want to cry," he'd say when I clouded up after skinning a knee, or, "You want to bring home some A's on your grade card," he'd tell me when I was inclined to give short shrift to my homework.

Now, when he said I wanted to go look in that spacious, hay-scented area we called the barn floor, I knew there was something important waiting there.

In a couple of minutes, I was out of my school dress and into my overalls, pumping my skinny legs down the long lane to the barn. I toed out the chock which kept the tall red barn door from hurting itself when the wind blew, put my shoulder against the end of the door, and grunted as I nudged open a space large enough for me to wriggle my skinny frame through sideways.

The yellow dog had heard me and was bouncing and barking at the end of a piece of Manila rope, where my Dad had tied him. He was a beautiful dog — perhaps, the most beautiful dog I had ever seen. The long hair of his back and sides, his hind legs, his perked-up ears and wildly flailing tail were bright, glistening red-brown, shot through with gold. A collar of long white hair ringed his neck, expanded into a pale chest, and extended to white front legs which were speckled with faint liver colored spots like those on his long, soft muzzle.

The dog jumped up and licked my face, and I scruffed his ears and slapped his sides, and I laughed out loud at his wildly gyrating tail. We stopped playing when Dad, who stood grinning in the doorway, said, "You want to let him loose, if you think you're going to keep him," so I untied my new dog.

The dog warden had sent word out to Daddy that morning that he had a young dog, nearly an adult, which might make a good farm animal and companion, and Daddy had driven to town to get him. A dollar and a half paid for his county license, was all the formality there had been to making him mine. My family agreed the dog had named himself "Bounce" with the greeting he'd given me when I entered the barn.

We never tried to learn anything about Bounce's past, but he was soon fitting into our way of life as though he had been born to it and, while he hadn't been adopted with any idea of his becoming a working dog, it wasn't long before he showed his eagerness to take on responsibility.

On a hundred-and-twenty-acre farm, there were chores enough for everyone and our days were ordered by the times when the jobs must be done. Chickens were fed and let in or out of their coops, horses were harnessed or put to pasture, sheep were watered, the garden was tended, housework was done, each in its proper time.

To me, the youngest member of the family, fell the easy duties of walking the quarter-mile south of home to the Washington Road, where our mailbox stood, to put out letters and wait for the mailman, and of bringing the cows from pasture for milking, twice a day. I carried endless pails of water to fill the sheep trough, and others to refresh Mama's flowerbeds and to scrub porches and sidewalks. I dawdled often to see how wild things grew and blossomed and made

178

seed; to discover where the bobwhite or the hen pheasant made her nest; to count the days until the chicks hatched and followed their mother from hiding. I wondered at the movement of clouds and shadows; and watched the snow, in winter, as it gathered and drifted and melted away.

Most often, Bounce was beside me, running when I ran, his tongue lolling, long flag of a tail waving excitedly. He sniffed eagerly through the past autumn's fallen leaves when springtime found us in a quiet woods, hunting sponge mushrooms.

On long summer days, the yellow dog and I often trod a quiet mile up an unpaved, untraveled road, to fish the Eagle Creek for bluegills and crappies. On such days, we shared lunch, a thick sandwich of bread and beans, and relished the taste of wild service berries or blackberries for dessert. He licked his chops and watched as I filled my cupped palms to catch sulphur-tainted water from an open spring in the nearby churchyard, waited while I slaked my own thirst, and then drank from my hands.

I marvel now that the child had no grasp of how those wonders would last to enrich the life of the adult.

One morning, when I left the house to go bring the cows from the pasture, I found the countryside shrouded in heavy fog. This early chore, before the school bus came, was familiar to both of us and Bounce was waiting for me by the kitchen door. By the time we reached the barn, I knew that finding fifteen or twenty cows, strung out over a forty-acre field, was going to be a problem, and I climbed to the top of the wooden pasture gate, hoping to figure out where the herd might be.

I could see no sign of the cows, and nothing reached my ears but the muffled drumming of the fog's moisture, dripping from the edges of the barn roof and falling into cold puddles on the ground. Resigned to the job, I climbed down from the gate and whistled for Bounce. The dog was nowhere to be seen.

"Here, Boy! Here, Bounce!" I called, again and again, but the dog had disappeared and I was faced with setting out alone. In that hardly-daylight hour, the thick, damp, clinging mist was spooky and made me leery of leaving the sheltering cluster of buildings, so I idled along, kicking at the fence row, hesitating to strike out into the open.

I had scuffed along for no more than ten or twenty yards when I heard the plodding footsteps of the cows and strained to peer into the fog. Blanche, the big black-and-white Holstein who always led the herd, materialized out of the gray curtain and, behind her came the rest of the milkers, all nicely bunched up and heading for the feedlot. As I ran to open the gate, I saw Bounce, trotting back and forth behind the herd, keeping the girls in line, like he was getting paid to do it.

With neither instruction nor command, he had sized up the situation and taken on a job which needed doing.

Once we had the herd penned in the lot that morning, Bounce and I celebrated what he had done with a quick scuffle. Then we ran all the way to the house with him barking his head off and me yelling for Dad and Mom to come and see what my dog had done.

Bounce had signed himself on as chief cow herder and, like any natural-born working dog, he seemed just pleased as he could be, to have found work. From that day forward, the asking was as good as the deed, though I think sometimes we probably confused him, as well as the cows, when we sent him to bring in the milkers at unaccustomed hours, just to show off his self-discovered ability to folks who dropped by in the middle of the day.

On another morning, it was my father who came bursting

through the kitchen door with an announcement about my dog's growing list of talents. "You'll never guess what Bounce just did," he said, as though he knew a secret.

Then, while my sister, Fern Louise, and I listened, open-mouthed, he told us how the dog had pointed a hen pheasant back on the line fence between our farm and that of our nearest neighbor to the east, Mac Frantz. Fern Louise and I weren't fully aware, at the time, what that might mean for, unlike many of our neighbors, Daddy was not an avid hunter.

In good time, Bounce would teach me about pointing gamebirds, and for those unfortunate souls who have never had the joy of exercising a good bird dog, let me explain: A "point" is made when a dog scents a gamebird. Sometimes the dog comes smack upon the bird, hugging the ground directly in his path; sometimes, the bird is slightly off to one side. In either case, the dog's motion is arrested at the moment of his first catching scent, often with a front paw raised in mid-stride, just like the pictures of bird dogs show it.

Nothing moves but the dog's head as its nose, as though pulled by an invisible string, is slowly drawn to the scent of the bird. The dog's nose is the "pointer"; his body and upraised paw remain facing whatever direction the dog was moving when he picked up the scent. When a dog and trainer are a good team, the dog stands motionless "on point" until his person locates the bird and flushes, or startles, it into flight. For a bird dog person, there are few sights more satisfying than a dog on point. And the human's excitement is most often secondary to that of the dog, when the deed is finished.

At the time Bounce revealed his talent for pointing, Hancock County, Ohio, was known as the ring-necked pheasant capital of the United States, and it would remain so

181

until the bad freeze of 1946 and '47 killed off many of the beautiful birds and the Dakotas took over the title. With the start of hunting season each year, bird hunters descended on the county like a plague and many of them took rooms in town, at the old Phoenix Hotel. They were in the field at daylight, hunted all day, and gathered back at the hotel's Pheasant Room after sundown, to toast their luck and tell each other about the tough shots they'd made and the easy ones they'd missed.

Word got out about what a good bird dog Bounce was and for many years, he was signed up on a regular basis and loaned out to find pheasants for the sportsmen from the big cities. Until I was old enough to hunt on my own, I followed along when it was neighbors who borrowed my dog.

When I heard about the field dog trials being organized in the northern part of the county one year, I coaxed my folks to let me enter Bounce. They consented, and it was with a great deal of pride and excitement that I walked up to the sign-in table and wrote down the names of my dog and me.

When it came Bounce's turn to locate pheasants, he didn't have a bit of trouble finding or holding his birds but, lacking the finesse and timing of the trained purebreds, he didn't win any ribbons. You couldn't have told it by mine or Bounce's reactions, however, for I was excited to see him show his stuff, and his own deportment was that of any working dog who knows the satisfaction of doing well a job he enjoys.

Winter had little effect on my wanting to spend time outdoors so, when snow lay deep upon the ground, Bounce and I often struck out across the fields to give him some practice. One morning, we left the barn and followed the fence rows northward, and then to the west, wading through the drifts close to the property line of our neighbor to the north. Bounce had made two or three good points when I began to feel the cold biting into my toes and fingers. Satisfied with the morning's exercise, the dog and I turned back to cut across the field toward home.

We'd gone only a hundred yards or so when Bounce, working in well-disciplined fashion fifteen or twenty feet ahead of me, began nervously zigzagging over the ground, his nose pushing up snow. I hurried to catch up with him and, at just about the same time, he and I both saw a small furrow, some four or five inches wide, making a bee-line through the snow.

Bounce was onto it in a flash, arrowing up the four- or five-foot long trail, which ended abruptly in a snowbank. The dog stopped and looked up into my face. "What is it?" I asked him.

He stood stiff-legged, his ears at attention, waiting for me to stop asking questions and tell him what to do. Bending over the place where the path ended in the snowbank, I could see a puff of brown fur beyond the spot where a cottontail's sudden stop had caused the snow to fall in a thin layer behind it.

I turned and looked into Bounce's excited face as I tried to decide what I should do, for this was the first time I would be faced with the life-or-death decision about an animal.

Hunting, for farmers, is a two-pronged proposition which covers the taking of food from his land and deals, also, with the necessity to maintain a healthy balance in the native wildlife living on his property, for those animals themselves form important links in the chain which makes nature work.

I stood up, stepped backward, took a deep breath, and said, "Come on, Bounce; let's go." I could tag along and watch adults fill the bulging game pockets on the backs of their hunting coats, but I was not yet ready to take responsibility for a creature's life.

Bounce cocked his head, with one ear raised questioningly, as I started to move away. Then, with a final sniff at the rabbit burrowed snugly into the snowdrift, he apparently put the incident behind him and ran with me across the field toward home.

My dad thought I should have let Bounce have his way with that rabbit, and I told him some other time, I might do just that.

When I was graduated from high school and moved to the city to begin making my fortune, Bounce stayed behind in the country. A year later, Mama died, and Daddy, in turn, moved to the city. Min and Charlie Marquart, who lived in the country south of the small village of Rawson, offered Bounce a place to live out his days, and we accepted.

From time to time, Daddy would drive up for a visit with Min and Charlie and I'd go along to walk back the cattle lane and into the woods with Bounce. It had been a while since we had done that when, one Sunday afternoon, I got the feeling I wanted to see my dog. My roommate offered to take me there, and we climbed into her old Plymouth coupe for the drive out to Min and Charlie's.

When we arrived, Betty Rayle stopped the car in the driveway and we got out. I didn't see Bounce, but I gave the simple two-note whistle I'd always used to call him. The old yellow dog came from the woodshed by the side of the house and loped down the hill. At about the halfway point, we met and fell to the ground, rough-housing as we had done hundreds of times before. Then, with a final face-licking by the dog and whacks to his ribs on my part, we stopped our play and I stood up to see Min and Charlie standing in the doorway, watching.

Charlie gulped a time or two, looked briefly up at the sky, cleared his throat, and said, "Mary Ellen, that dog hain't been

184

out of that woodshed for three days. If I'da knowed where to get you, I'da called you up and asked you to come and see him. I think he's been lookin' for you."

I knew what Charlie was trying to say. I believe, somehow, I'd known it when I decided to go there that day. I wasn't sorry for the rough way we'd played, even if it had taken a lot of the old dog's meager reserve of strength; I knew our companionship meant as much to Bounce as it did to me. I stayed as long as I felt welcome allowed that afternoon, and rode quietly back to town.

I called Charlie in the middle of the week to ask about Bounce.

"It was an odd thing," said the old farmer. "Monday morning, he got up and kind of shook himself off at the woodshed door and headed for that open gate by the side of the cowbarn. I said to Min, 'Looky there; he hain't done that in a couple-a weeks.'" Charlie was talking with a lump in his throat and I was glad we weren't face to face, for he'd always considered himself a tough old bird.

"I walked out in the yard, where I could see what he was doing," Charlie continued. "I watched him walk down the cattle lane, sniffing the fence row, like he always used to do, only a lot slower. He was about halfway to the woods when a cock pheasant hollered and I seen it fly up. Bounce watched it fly away and then just stopped and looked back at me for a little bit, and turned around and laid down, right there, in the middle of the lane. He was dead by the time I got to him, but he didn't suffer. He was a good old dog and he never forgot what it was to run a fence row, lookin' for pheasants."

I haven't owned a dog since Bounce; I would be hard put to find another full-of-surprises, untrained, all-purpose dog, as he had turned out to be.

It is only since I began to tell his story that I gave some thought to comparing his looks with any purebred working dog. I dug out a picture I'd taken one Sunday afternoon when Bounce and I had walked down to Eagle Creek together, and held it up beside one of the portraits in a dog book. I was pleasantly surprised to see that his conformation, his stance, the set of his head and ears, even his coloring, were almost identical to the textbook picture of the Border Collie tri-color, a breed of which, in my youth, I had no knowledge.

*   *   *   *   *

I'd met other working dogs, here and there, over the years, but I'd never known one who actually had a part in a moving picture, until I heard that a dog friend of mine, Kerry, had made a video. Kerry is a Border Collie, member of the large family of pedigreed working dogs which includes all of the herders and cattle dogs, the trackers and draft dogs, the hunting and racing hounds, and the sportsmen's breeds, known as gundogs.

The Border Collie is one of the world's oldest lines but, because its owners and breeders believe that breeding for appearance is detrimental to the work ethic natural to the Border Collie, a standard of appearance was slow to be established. Only recently has a very liberal standard been accepted by a representative group of breeders and the American Kennel Club and, for many people, the breed will continue to be considered the epitome of working dogs, regardless of show points.

The Border Collie line came, probably, from the

186

combining of the large, fierce dogs which accompanied the Romans when they invaded the British Isles in the First Century B.C., with the smaller dogs which traveled there in the Viking invasion of the Eighth Century A.D. Their name came from the fact that the best workers of the breed, originally known as Collies, have always seemed to come out of the counties on the border of northern England and southern Scotland.

Rated the most intelligent of all domestic breeds, the Border Collie has a natural adaptability to such work as search and rescue, particularly after earthquake and avalanche; for sheep and cattle herding; for personal protection, guard, and guide services; for tracking, and for retrieval of downed game. Border Collie teams have been winners in sled dog racing on the North American continent, as well as in England. They are keenly amenable to discipline. Their eagerness to please, their inborn acceptance of responsibility, and their desire to work, place them at the top of the charts as performers in motion picture production and in other fields of entertainment.

Rena Blomé had been brought up in a family for whom underdog rescue was an important fact of everyday life. When she married a fellow teacher, Merrill Stevens, who shared her philosophy about animals, the two of them continued to take in strays until a visit to the British Isles, in 1981, offered a new slant to their idea of a family dog.

"There were Border Collies everywhere," Rena remembers. "I was just so impressed with the way they worked at whatever they were doing. We saw them in the cities, and all over the country and, when we went into the northern part of England, then Ireland, and on, into Scotland, we saw them herding sheep. We were both just completely taken by the way those dogs worked and, especially, by the bond which was so obvious between every one of the dogs and its master. I said right then that if we ever had a pedigreed dog, I wanted it to be a Border Collie, and Merrill agreed."

Rena and Merrill realized they should not fulfill their dream for such a dog as long as both of them were away from home every weekday, and while their hope was postponed, they gave sanctuary and loving care to sundry castoff, orphaned, or ill-used dogs.

Then, just before Christmas of the year Rena had opted for an early retirement, her mother's old schnauzer died and Rena began visiting the SPCA and watching the newspaper want-ads in search of a replacement. Scanning the ads one day, she spotted just what she was looking for: a small adult dog which would be a suitable companion for her mother. And then something unexpected happened.

Just below the Home Wanted ad was a notice about Border Collie puppies for sale.

Rena quickly checked out the older dog, decided it was just right, and delivered it to her mother's home. When Merrill came from school that day, Rena was standing in the driveway, waiting to go see the puppies.

The standard Border Collie is black with a white collar which extends to the dog's chest and front legs with, most often, some white about the face and muzzle. Borders are also bred as "reds" and "tricolors," which contain black, shades of red-brown, and white. There may be some mottling of the dog's darker color found in the white of its face and legs.

When Rena and Merrill arrived at Kandy Robinson's kennel, in Clearwater, Florida, they found that, from the litter of six, only two puppies remained, one male and a female. Kandy explained that those which were gone had been chosen for various reasons of personal preference, primarily color, as many owners prefer the red-brown highlighting with which some members of the litter had been born.

The Stevenses, however, had their minds set upon a black-and-white with a speckled face, for they relished that as the true look of the breed. The spirited little eight-week-old male was just that, and the decision to take him home was mutual and immediate. They registered the puppy as Merena's Kerry Ross, and called him Kerry, for the county in Ireland where they had become so enamored of the breed.

Kerry's training began immediately, as he quickly accepted a large wire enclosure in the Stevens' living room as his own personal space from which, when his family were at home, he could come and go as he pleased. Closed into it at night and when his family was away, it helped in housebreaking him, for the Border Collie, like most dogs, will not soil the place where he sleeps.

During his first two weeks with the Stevenses, Kerry learned the confines of his new home and fenced yard and began to feel secure in a household where he was loved and played with and well cared for.

And then it was time for school. Rena enrolled him in Kandy Robinson's Kindergarten Puppy Training, or KPT, where, one day a week for eight weeks, he was exposed to experiences which would teach him not to fear strangers, loud noises, or unexpected changes in people — things like large hats and unusual clothing. His familiarity with his own name was reinforced, and he learned to come when called.

It was an inauspicious beginning for a pup whose great-great-grandfather, on his father's side, a Scot, had been an International Herding Champion, and whose mother had come from a fine old Southern family, Americans for five generations.

189

From his four weeks in puppy school, where he learned to curb such fun activities as jumping up on people and nibbling their hands or ankles, Kerry went directly into an eight weeks' course called Basic Obedience. There he learned to sit, to stay, and to lie down on command, not to go out when a door was left open, and other good dog manners.

This was followed by an open-ended course called Sub-novice, which would take Kerry to the threshold of competitive training. Even though the Stevenses did not intend making a competition show dog of Kerry, they wanted him to have the benefit — and the fun — of continued training. The rapidly maturing dog took to every level of training with enthusiasm and an unflaunting desire to please.

"Thursday evening, when we went to class," Rena says, "was his favorite time of the week. 'You want to go to school?' I'd ask him, and he'd race for the door, happy as a little boy with his first new book satchel."

Graduating to Novice training, Kerry began to add the finesse of American Kennel Club requirements to the points of obedience he had already acquired. Performing extended stays and sit-stays, down-stays, and walking in the AKC prescribed heel position, all became a part of his behavior.

I had first seen Kerry as an eager, fuzzy, little pup, thrusting his face from the open car window, tongue-first, when Rena stopped in front of my house to show him off. It was love at first sight for me, too, and throughout his early training, it was sometimes almost more than I could manage to resist joining the two of them at practice at their end of our short street.

To my credit, I did not nib into his lessons. At the same time, I felt especially honored on those occasions when the dog brought me his saliva coated toys to toss for his retrieving. The first time I approached the Stevens' house when they weren't home and heard Kerry's warning bark cease as he recognized my voice, I knew my status had been elevated to friend of the dog.

I was curious about all his training, and wondered if a dog which was headed for full-time work as a sheep or cattle herder would be schooled this way.

"No," Rena said. "His education would be in a different vein. Most people who have working dogs believe their dogs should have less obedience training. They think it makes the dog too dependent upon the owner or handler for direction. They want their dogs, when they're working stock, to think for themselves."

"You're making a city dog of Kerry," I inferred; "an intelligent dog who will be happy, well-cared for, and know that he is secure in his situation — a good citizen."

"That's right. I saw that Kerry's obedience trainer was driving a hundred miles, three or four times a week, to put her dogs on sheep, and, at the same time, was following through with their obedience training. A lot of people don't do that, but she was successfully giving her dogs both courses, and I saw what happy dogs she had. I realized, once again, that these dogs must have something to do. You cannot just take one home and put it into a pen and take it for walks, now and then."

"A working dog is a happy dog?"

"Exactly. And it doesn't make any difference what the work is. He must have work."

"Has Kerry been on sheep?"

A proud, thought-you'd-never-ask grin exploded on Rena's face, as she reached for a photograph I'd missed on a nearby table. She handed it over to me.

I bit hard on a thumbnail and felt that tightness in my chest which always occurs when I see any animal doing what its master wants done. The photograph was of Kerry, sweet and low down in a half crouch, head firmly forward in line with his backbone, his brown eyes fixed on a pair of ewes hoofing for the gate, just ahead.

"How many times had he done this?" I asked, and I made no effort to hide my amazement over this new facet of Kerry's behavior.

Rena, likewise, wasn't covering up her feelings when she answered, "That was the first time, and he did it perfectly."

Like anyone else who has trod the halls of academia, Kerry is a "lettered" individual; the initials CD, for Companion Dog, and CGD for Canine Good Citizenship, now rightfully follow his name. And he is training, simultaneously, to add a TD, for Tracking Dog, and a CDX for Companion Dog Excellent, to those titles. Merrill and Rena Stevens insist, and I know it is true, that outside the classroom Kerry has clung to the designation SRD for Spoiled Rotten Dog for, with all his training, he is still a robust and loving family pet.

Kerry

I count Rena and Merill Stevens among my friends, but I think it has become obvious to them as well as to me that, frequently, my visits to their home are made for the sole purpose of spending some time with a fine dog who is proud of his calling.

One afternoon, as Rena and I chatted, with Kerry lying between our two chairs, she wondered, casually, if she'd remembered to tell me about Kerry's video. I said she hadn't, and thought, as she continued, how totally like Rena it was to keep to herself something which, if it had happened in my family, soon would have been a common-knowledge item.

Kerry's current trainer had called, one day, Rena said, to ask whether she and Kerry would be available for something rather special on the following Monday.

"Special, like what?" my friend wanted to know.

"Well, I have scheduled another client's dog to do a commercial video that day," said the trainer. "I've been given a list of the things the dog will have to do and I know Kerry can do all of them. I'd like for you to bring Kerry along as back-up."

Rena agreed and, on the appointed day, she and Kerry drove to a nearby suburb where a newly occupied, upscale private home had been selected for the filming. Soon after their arrival, the trainer told Rena the director had decided Kerry was just the sort of dog he wanted for the video and without any special preparation, Kerry found himself before the floodlights.

Throughout the afternoon, it was as though Kerry had been born to the stage. As dropped lines and miscalculations on the part of the human actors made retakes necessary, the dog, over and over again, acted on cue. He responded to Rena's silent signals to come, sit, or stay, his innate curiosity and desire to please lending a natural and believable polish to his performance.

When the director announced that the production was a wrap — industry parlance for "finished" — he displayed amazement that the video had been Kerry's first experience before a camera and offered Rena the business card of an animal actors' agent who might be interested in an interview.

Some time later, my heart was full as I watched the

finished video. Kerry, of course, stole the show. I do remember the products which were being displayed for future showing at trade fairs, but I'd be hard put to describe a single actor, other than Kerry, who appeared in the production.

Throughout the performance as, indeed, is obvious in everything Kerry and his kind do, there is never the slightest doubt that, as Rena Stevens says, "Whatever he is being asked to do is just exactly what he wants to do, right that moment."

Just as apparent is the maxim I have heard from men and women who own and work pedigreed Border Collies from Scotland to England to Texas, and have seen in those untrained pet dogs of my own past, dogs through whose veins, perhaps, some of the same blood flowed — A working dog is a happy dog.

HORSE MAN

Bill and Bob

From the time he was old enough to tie the reins around his waist and follow a single-bottom plow, Frank George was a horse man, which is somewhat different from being a horseman.

"Horseman" seems to imply a mere mastery of horses; having, perhaps, a power over them, an ability to persuade these largest of domestic animals to do one's bidding.

"Horse man," on the other hand, suggests, for me at least, a deep caring for horses: a feeling about their moods and strengths. It speaks of recognizing their will and their huge heart, of working with those qualities, and of the animals' being as much a part of one's life as the people known by the man and the place he inhabits.

Frank George was such a person and, as his foster child, I know that he had — though he never would have put such a name to it — a love for the great beasts which worked with him, provided entertainment for his leisure time, and were a source of pride throughout his life.

The year was 1894. A mile north of Ada, Ohio, in a log cabin which was later added to and modernized somewhat,

Frank was born to Thomas and Rebecca George, the youngest of their two boys and three girls who survived.

As a boy, Frank rode a little horse down the road to classes at the Brown Schoolhouse, about a mile from home. There he would dismount, slap the horse on the rump, and send it home. In the afternoon, when school was over for the day, the horse would be waiting by the school pump; Rebecca would have sent it to fetch home her favorite child.

In spite of her aspirations for him, Rebecca lost to her husband's iron will the battle to keep her boy in school; when he had finished the third year of his formal education, his father did not allow him to return. His brother, Gene, fifteen years older, had already left home to work aboard the ore boats on the Great Lakes, and Tom George saw earnest little Frankie as his only chance of a helper he could groom to take over the work of the farm. And the sooner the better.

Tom preferred a necktie and carefully blackened shoes to the open necked shirt and dusty brogans of a working farmer, but such garb suited the boy just fine. As a result, Frank's first dress coat and spats were a long time coming.

The boy seemed to have been born knowing the ways of horses and it became his second nature to follow a team through the seasons of plowing, planting, weeding, and harvesting. Thomas George gradually shifted work and responsibility to his son until, as a young man, Frank was shouldering responsibility for the 200-acre farm. When his physical growth stopped, he was five feet eleven inches tall, with a powerful body which would be strong and muscular for the rest of his life.

From Rebecca's Pennsylvania Dutch background, Frank developed honesty, endurance, and a drive for achievement so, in addition to the hard work at home, he hired himself out on local jobs. Taking orders from other bosses was a welcome change and the income, squirreled away, offered the hope of one day being on his own.

Frank and his first team of horses — a fine matched pair of black geldings — soon became known and respected throughout Hardin County as being worth their hire. He had raised the two from colts, working out their ownership on what would remain, in spite of his labor, his father's farm.

During the second decade of the twentieth century, industries and the cities it took to support them were growing by leaps and bounds; roads and railroads were spidering through the Ohio farmland. The towns demanded a building boom, also, of new homes and whole new blocks of commercial buildings.

The last time I drove through Ada with Daddy, he recalled those times and pointed out buildings he'd had a part in building. Leaning forward slightly to look toward the time-darkened facade of a pre-World War I business structure, he said, with pride, "I hauled the stone for that whole block a' buildings," and as we drove past the fine old homes on Main Street, "Bill and Bob skidded out the timber for the beams in that house."

The rock and stone Frank and his team had hauled had come from Grant Tressel's quarries, one of which is the gaping hole in the ground which I remember as being in the front lawn of Great Uncle Grant and Great Aunt Della's mansion at the north end of town. The lumber they took to the mills in town had been harvested in the wood lots of surrounding farms.

Southeast of town, Daddy pointed across a meadow which stretched from the roadside to the horizon. "That was all woods, back when Bill and Bob, and me was skiddin' logs," he said. "One morning, I was to go in there and haul timber to town. It was colder'n hell, and Paw said I wasn't to go; I'd

197

kill my horses if I did. Nevertheless...." I'm still surprised by his use of that word. "Nevertheless, I went. I knew my team better'n Paw did, and they did their day's work, just like I knowed they would."

Daddy never tired of talking about Bill and Bob and I never tired of listening.

"The biggest log we ever hauled out of the woods was an oak log, and it had over thirteen hundred board feet in it. It was the biggest log that went in to the Ada mill in sixteen years. We hauled it off of Uncle Chester Thompson's place, east of Bluffton. From it and another tree cut down at the same time, Bill and Bob and me hauled seven loads out of the woods."

* * * * *

It was a spry little horse named Nell which pulled Frank's buggy when he courted and won the heart of Emma Tressel, in 1917. (Fifteen years later, Frank and Emma would take my sister Fern and me from the children's home, in Hancock County, and become our daddy and mama.)

Mama used to tell me she always dreaded the buggy ride home from church services on Sunday morning, when someone was sure to challenge her young man and his horse to a race. Never one to hold a horse back if it wanted to run, she said, Frank would give the reins a flick and Nell would high-tail it for home. With Mama hanging on to her bonnet with one hand and to the buggy for dearlife with the other, they would clatter over ruts and potholes and take the eastward turn off of Route 69 on two wheels, heading for Albert Tressel's place.

The noise of their arrival would bring Emma's parents, Dora and Albert, into the yard: Dora, to escort this second-youngest of their seven pretty daughters into the house, and Albert, to roundly denounce his future son-in-law for his carelessness and lack of responsibility. Out of sight and hearing of the ladies, however, it was another matter, for then Albert would require a full description of the race and all of its participants, with an account of just whose horses little Nell had outpaced.

*   *   *   *   *

Throughout his lifetime, Frank George worked mostly heavy teams but, now and then, he'd come by a smaller horse which had the grit required of a good workhorse.

Prince and Ben, blacks I remember from childhood, were that kind of small, wily horse. Each of them was bought as a single to work with other horses and, because of their similar size and disposition, became a team. Ben, bought at public auction, wore an indecipherable brand on his left hip, and Daddy was always prideful of the fact he believed him to have been a range horse.

Ben was a strong and willing worker. Never totally trustworthy as to temperament, however, he was the only horse we children were ever forbidden to approach. The wisdom of this was borne out when Ralph Lanning, the landlady's common-law husband, surprised Ben and was kicked to the stable floor for his lack of care. The horse man, however, exacted full days of hard work from the rascally creature and rewarded the rambunctious animal's effort with extra portions of corn or oats.

Ike was another of Daddy's "little" horses, but one I only

199

heard of, as he was before my time.

"Ike was a standard bred horse, and he could run, but he wasn't fast enough for the money. I bought him for Thirty-nine Dollars and worked him nine years, and sold him for Forty. He was a sulky horse, but I worked him just like a draft horse. As far as these little horses is concerned, to go out and work a load, most of them couldn't lug a load like a heavy horse could. Ike could do it. If I wanted to put a hundred bushel of corn on a wagon and haul it, I did it and Ike, he pulled it. But there's one thing you got to remember: It takes just as much feed to feed a little horse as it does a big one."

After he and Mama moved to Hancock County, where he farmed 120 acres, Daddy always aimed at keeping two teams and a spare, which gave him latitude in shifting them about when there was heavy work to be done day after day. Daddy asked for and got a lot from his horses, but he was a great believer in letting them have a day off.

*   *   *   *

The second horse Daddy owned and named Nellie was a light colored mare with a silver mane and tail; her teammate was a darker horse named Queen. Nellie was gentle and trustworthy for hitching to the garden plow or for bridling on a Sunday afternoon when city cousins wanted to ride.

The months after it became known, one summer, that Nellie was to bring a colt, were times of excitement. Daddy was sure the colt would be a gray, like its sire; Mama was just as sure the baby would have Nellie's coloring, and a typical country wager was struck: a new pair of bib overalls if Daddy won, a new dress if Mama was right.

By noon on the day of her labor, Daddy was sure Nellie was in trouble and, when he moved her from her stall into the open barn floor, a mood of deep apprehension settled over all of us. By late afternoon Daddy had decided he needed the vet, and went to Reed Elsea's place, just south of us, to telephone for help. Close to nightfall Doc Hall came, unbending his long frame as he climbed out of the car and walked toward the barn.

For my sister and me, Doc Hall's presence was as good as a sentence of death, for Doc was summoned the ten miles from his office in town only when some problem with the stock was considered beyond Daddy's doctoring. Most often, and not necessarily due to anything lacking in Doctor Hall's capabilities, a call to the reduction company for removal of the animal's carcass was made when the veterinarian departed.

Fern Louise, 7, and I, 5 years old at the time, were told to stay in the house, from where we watched, our noses pressed to the glass in the dining room door, though all we could see of Nellie's struggle through the dark hours was an occasional movement of the coal oil lantern behind the partly open barn door. Far into the night we watched, hope rising and falling each time Daddy came to the house for coffee, or hot water, or supplies, or just to give Mama a report of Nellie's progress.

It was nearly dawn when we saw Doc Hall get into his car, turn it around in the barnyard, and drive slowly up the long driveway, past the house, and out to the road.

With heavy steps, Daddy trudged up the lane and came in to tell us that our beloved Nellie had died. The foal, however, was alive. Mama dug out a bottle and a large, black rubber nipple which we used in springtime to feed disowned lambs, warmed a dipper of milk, and went to the barn with Daddy to feed the orphan colt.

The pale, spindly-legged, strawberry colt, colored like neither of his parents, but a combination of both, was named Johnny. In spite of every good intention to the contrary, he became a spoiled pet and, although he broke to harness and exhibited the gentle disposition of his dam, he was never a totally reliable draft horse, as Nellie had been.

*   *   *   *   *

The decade of the thirties was well advanced when, early one morning, a neighbor drove Daddy to a farm near Benton Ridge, some ten miles away, to buy the big team of Belgian mares which were to be the last horses he would own. Astride first one and then the other, testing their temperament, he rode the pair home, arriving in time for noon dinner.

Pet and Tops had grown up together from birth, had been broken to harness together, and had worked as a team on a single farm for most of their ten years.

"They weighed a ton apiece and wore twenty-four-inch collars, and they were as good a team of horses as I ever owned. There wasn't nothing they wouldn't pull, if you told 'em to, and all they needed was a word. I could drop the reins and they'd walk a straight line. They were the only team I could ever trust to pull a load of hay into the mow without me havin' ahold of the reins, and they knew just how far to walk, for me to trip the hayfork."

Though unmatched in color, for Pet was a red roan and Tops a strawberry roan, they were equal in size and conformation. If there was any difference at all between

202

them, it was no more than a slight refinement in Pet's gentle attitude toward people. She was always the choice to be harnessed for any job which required but a single horse, and was the favorite when they were bridled for Sunday afternoon riding.

"You never saw a quieter horse than Pet, when there was children around. She'd stand perfectly still, and she'd turn her head and look, to see where they were and what they were doing, before she'd commence to move."

Pet and Tops could be ground-tied, in harness, like well-trained saddle horses; they could be turned out with other stock without a second thought, and they had not the slightest fear of machinery or any of the other farm animals. When my favorite cat was ready to bring forth kittens, it was often in a corner of the hay box of one of these giants that Fluff made her nest.

In winter they pulled a cumbersome, wooden, V-shaped drag, to clear snow from the eighth of a mile of driveway which led from the road to the barn, and the quarter-mile of gravel road which would allow us and our nearest neighbors access to a main road.

Their springtime steps defined furrows for the plow, the disk, the harrow, and then the planter. In summer, their heavy feet trod carefully between the rows of growing corn without damaging a single plant. Come fall, they measured the rows again, as they pulled the binder which cut and tied the heavy stalks into manageable sheaves. Then, more leisurely, with the reins looped around the wagon stake and working only from the sound of Daddy's voice, they pulled a wagon to gather the ears of corn as they were husked by hand from the shocks.

The years of World War II were times of many shortages, when folks made do, for the most part, with what they had. The big team's harness, then, was old and, time and again, I would be attracted to the ring of hammer on anvil, and would run to watch as Daddy spliced the aging leather straps with hand-flattened copper, or the harder brass, rivets. Eventually, the harness reached the point it could no longer hold a mend.

"I had the money, but I couldn't buy new harness, because it wasn't to be had, so I called a fella out from over by Lima to make a new set of harness. He came out and measured the horses and went back home and made the harness, and he charged me sixty-five dollars for them. When he delivered the harness, he had made each one of you girls a little white leather collar with nickel silver studs on it, for your pet lambs. That was something. Those lamb collars were worth the price of the harness to you and Fern."

When wheat and oats ripened in the hot sun of July and August, Pet and Tops experienced the nearest they ever approached to a social season, for it was the one time of year they had an opportunity to hobnob among others of their own kind.

Fred Inbody and his four sons, neighbors whose farm was located three or four miles north and west of our place, owned one of the noisy behemoths called threshing machines. Dan Clevenger and his four boys, whose farm lay about as far away in the opposite direction, owned another. Every summer, each of these men signed up a "ring" of a dozen or so farmers, all of whom would help with the others' threshing, as the rig was moved from farm to farm. By the middle of summer, Daddy would have signed up with one or the other of these groups.

Early each morning during the season, Daddy walked Pet and Tops the three or four or more miles to whatever farm was being worked. There, they and the other teams hauled the wagonloads of dried sheaves from the field to the threshing machine, which would have been positioned wherever the farmer wanted to situate his strawstack. The bundles were forked from the wagons onto a wood-slatted, canvas conveyer belt which carried them into the separator, where the grain was "threshed" from its stalks and seed coverings.

The crumpled, empty stalks were deposited by the machine into a stack which grew steadily on one side of the machine, to become winter bedding for the farm's livestock. At another point, the separator spewed a golden cascade of grain into a wagon to be hauled to the farmer's grainary. Beneath the machine, meanwhile, grew a smaller pile of "chaff," the dusty refuse of the process.

"I mind the time Dan Clevenger's threshing machine got stuck in a mudhole, and there wasn't a tractor around could pull it out. I said, 'Here, let me hitch old Pet and Tops to the son-of-a-bitch,' and they walked off with it without even bellyin' down."

At day's end, the team would trod home again, bringing one of the most welcome sounds of my childhood. By ear, I would follow the progress of the wagon on the nearest quarter-section road which paralleled ours, listening for the scrunch of the steel-rimmed wheels when they turned onto the blacktopped Washington Road. Then, bare feet and dress tail flying, I would set off to meet Daddy, running for all I was worth. By the time we met, he and the team would have made the final turn toward home and would be traveling the last quarter-mile of gravel.

Daddy would slow the team to let me run alongside, acting as though he didn't intend to let me ride. Some days he would stop and I would climb aboard the wagon, using for a high step the two-by-four which stuck out at the rear of the wagon. Other days became, suddenly, very special days when he'd yell, "Climb up on Ol' Pet!" Then he'd slow the team till they were barely moving and watch while I'd put my foot into the breeching strap and grab for the hames knob to scramble up to the horse's broad back. There, I would ride in imagined circusian splendor, inhaling the pungent odors of the horse's sweat and breath, all mixed with the sweet smell of the windblown chaff which clung to Pet's dark mane.

Bushels of grain to the acre and the size of a farm's strawstack, those days, were items to be considered when reckoning a farmer's effectiveness.

"I hear some of these fellas today, they talk about straw and fodder and they don't know the difference. A strawstack was oats or wheat straw, and it was used for bedding for the stock. They ain't no strawstacks any more. It's all left out on the field, to be plowed in under. Fodder come from corn. It was the stalks and the leaves, and it stayed in the field, in shocks, after we shucked the ears out. We hauled the fodder in by the wagonload, as we needed it, for feed."

"Some people cut their corn green and run it through a silin' machine and put it in a silo. It kinda soured in the silo, and they called it silage or ensilage and fed it to the cows like that. Your Uncle Chester used to do that. But it was an awful poor farmer that ever fed any straw to his livestock."

On winter mornings, after breaking the ice in the watering

tank so the stock could drink, Daddy opened the stable door and Pet and Tops came out into the barnyard. Tossing their great heads and snorting at the cold, they walked stiff-legged to the tank, their warm breath smoking around their faces before evaporating in the frigid air. Cold though it was, they always splashed their muzzles in the water a while before drinking and then, after slurping deep draughts of the icy water, they would wheel and run for the pasture gate which had already been pulled aside.

Well-toned muscles flexed and rolled; iron shoes thundered on the frozen sod, as Pet and Tops pounded through the gate and ran, manes and tails flying, around a circle of the 35-acre pasture.

It was a familiar routine, seen and heard so many mornings I can hear, like it was now, the whuff, whuff, whuff, made by their breath and the movement of their great bodies as they ran. From a rung of the pasture fence where I could stretch to see them turn in the far corner of the field and pound their way back, I shouted to them out of the naked joy I felt in the beauty of the huge beasts' running.

One such morning, as the pair dashed through the gate, Pet's left hind foot skidded on a small patch of ice, where a puddle of water always stood after a rain, and the leg skewed crazily outward. The horse could not recover her balance and went down heavily on her right side. She whinnied briefly and floundered for only a moment, then struggled to her feet and loped into the field toward Tops, who had stopped to wait for her.

They ran a little way together, slowed to a walk, stood quietly for a few moments, and returned to the barn.

I turned to Daddy, who had been called from the barn by the sound of Pet's whinny, and told him what had happened. "She's walking," he said. "She'll be all right. If she gets sore,

I'll rub some linament on it. She'll be all right."

But when he approached her and stroked the hip she was favoring, a worried look came over his face and, grasping a wisp of her dark mane, he led her into the barn floor and gave her a pan of oats.

Throughout the day, Pet stood in the barn, refusing to put weight on her right hind leg, while neighbors came to look and to comment and to care. That night, I carried water to her, and she drank. I held handfuls of sweet hay to her muzzle, and she ate. And I hoped she might be getting well.

The next morning, she was down in the center of the barn floor, and neither Daddy's urgings nor the nickering of Tops from her nearby stall could bring Pet to her feet.

It was time to call Doc Hall.

The vet confirmed that Pet's hip was broken and said she should be stood up and raised high enough to keep her from putting any weight on it. Our neighbor, Mac Frantz, had come as soon as his own chores were finished that morning. Now, while his grandson, Wayne, and I watched, the men carefully worked the lines of the hay sling under the suffering horse.

When the lines were all fastened and reeved through a pulley over the place where Pet lay, Tops was harnessed and led from her stall. As she reached the open barn floor, she stopped by the side of her lifelong mate and looked down at her.

Daddy let the big strawberry roan stand there for a moment, then urged her forward and hitched her to the lines he'd rigged over Pet.

"All right, Tops," he said quietly, and the trustworthy Belgian took up the slack in the lines. But as she felt the first strain on her harness, Tops relaxed, stopped, and turned to look back at the other horse.

Mac Frantz was the first to find his voice. "She ain't gonna do it, Frank. By God, she knows that old horse is hurtin', and she ain't gonna do it."

"Yes, she will," replied Daddy, as he gave a slight flex to the reins. "Come on, Tops; pull," he urged quietly.

Once more, Tops began to put her muscle into the harness, but once more, she relaxed and turned, and Pet returned the look. There's nothing for it but to say it was the saddest look I ever saw pass between two animals.

Now, understand. It was not that Tops could not move Pet; it was simply that she would not do it. Tears streamed down my face and, as Tops again strained slightly and relaxed, Pet reached to grasp at the hay with her lips and then let it drop as her head fell to one side. The faithful heart of the great and beautiful horse had stopped.

Doc Hall drove back to town and Mac Frantz promised to call the reduction company from the telephone at his house.

*   *   *   *   *

Tops remained on the farm, and worked with other horses until Daddy stopped farming after the end of World War II. A farmer Daddy knew, named Rupright, took Tops home to his own farm and promised she would end her days in gentle retirement.

*   *   *   *   *

Frank George never outgrew his love of horses. After he left the farm and moved into town he cared from time to time for a string of sulky horses belonging to his friends, the Greenos. And he became close friends with Doctor

Schoonover, the vet who owned BiLou and the speckled dog, Popcorn. One of the last places I ever went with Daddy was the Schoonover farm, where he walked among the skittish horses, patting a familiar hip or neck and saying a quiet word to old friends.

Not long after he entered his 89th year, I spent my last day with Daddy, in a hospital room. He came irregularly in and out of consciousness, and there was not much for me to do but to sit and remember and let my love go out to him, unacknowledged. I knew the end was not far away for Daddy, and I was glad for the times I had called him, triggered the telephone answering machine to record our conversation, and plied him with questions about things I wanted to hear again and keep forever.

Suddenly, that day, he struggled to raise his head from the pillow, and looked toward the hospital room's door, from which some hallway noise must have invaded his rest. A look of excitement came over his thin, ashen face. He turned toward me, squinting, as his eyes swept across the ceiling. "Why, that was Fluff," he said.

"You mean old Fluff?" I asked, remembering the cat who had been with us for thirteen years of my childhood.

"Yes, old Fluff," he answered. "She's been dead a long time."

In a little while, he wrenched his head and shoulders to one side as though trying to avoid being struck by something. "Ketch them horses! They're runnin' off!" he rasped.

His head fell back to the pillow, and quiet came over his face again. With other thoughts and worries beyond him, the memories of the animals which had peopled his life had returned to the old horse man.